THE BRIDESMAID'S SECRET

BY

SOPHIE WESTON

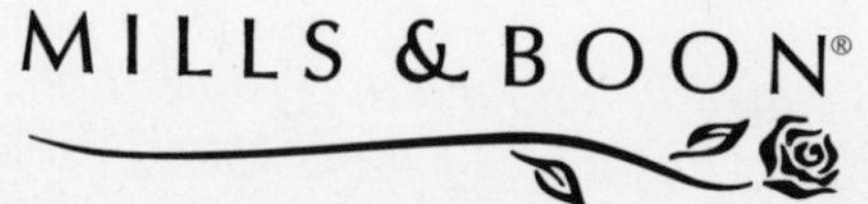

First published in Great Britain 2001
Large Print edition 2002
Harlequin Mills & Boon Limited,
Eton House, 18-24 Paradise Road,
Richmond, Surrey TW9 1SR

ISBN 0 263 17265 1

Set in Times Roman 16 on 18½ pt.
16-0102-52767

Printed and bound in Great Britain
by Antony Rowe Ltd, Chippenham, Wiltshire

CHAPTER ONE

'OF COURSE Bella will be your bridesmaid. Why on earth wouldn't she?'

Annis shuffled sample wedding invitations uneasily. 'Oh, I don't know,' she said vaguely. 'She's only been in New York a couple of months. Maybe she'd prefer to settle in properly before making a major trip back to London.'

'Sure,' said Bella's mother. 'That's why she didn't come back at Christmas. But your *wedding*. That's different. She's been waiting to be your bridesmaid all her life.'

Annis smiled reluctantly. 'You're right there. Bella was born to wear flowers in her hair.'

Instinctively they both looked at the photograph on the bookcase. It was a black and white studio portrait, all cheekbones and soulful eyes. So it missed the gold in Bella's hair or the forget-me-not blue of those eyes. But what it caught completely was the *fun*. The eyes sparkled. There was a naughty tilt to the head. You could tell that, in spite of her solemn pose and the dramatic lighting, laughter was on the point of breaking through. This was a girl who thought life was a party and who wasn't going to sit still much longer while it went on without her.

Lynda Carew smiled on her absent daughter. 'Yes, she still loves dressing up, doesn't she?'

'Hey, we can't call it dressing up any more. Now she's working for *Elegance Magazine*, she's a high-fashion babe.'

Lynda suppressed a sigh. 'She's certainly found herself the ideal job. I just wish she hadn't had to go so far away to get it.'

Annis had a feeling that the miles between the Carews' London home and *Elegance Magazine*'s Manhattan office was a good part of the reason that Bella had so surprisingly applied for the job in the first place. She did not say so. What was a feeling, after all? Just a faint impression, based on a couple of things Bella had said months ago, which Annis had paid no attention to at the time. Coupled with the things she had *not* said when Annis had announced that she was marrying Kosta Vitale.

And then that abrupt departure for the US.

But, on the other hand, Bella always did things on the spur of the moment. Miss Spontaneous, that was what her stepfather called her. And she had always been a globe-trotter.

The wedding preparations list forgotten, Annis tapped her teeth with her pen. Heck, maybe it was nothing. Feelings had never been her strong point. It was Bella who understood why people did things, not Annis, the intellectual stepsister she called Brain Box.

'Annis—'

She looked up. Lynda was watching her narrowly. Annis blinked. She loved and respected her stepmother but it was still sometimes a bit of a shock to bump into one of her moments of shrewdness.

'Is there something I should know?' Lynda asked quietly.

It was a question Annis had dreaded for weeks. Partly because she did not know the answer. Partly because sometimes—in the early morning when Kosta was still sleeping and she was awake and dreamily content in his arms—she half wondered if her happiness had somehow been bought at Bella's expense. She did not quite see how that could have happened. But there was *something*—

'No,' she said now uncertainly.

Lynda was not a dragon but when something was important she did not give up easily.

'Is something wrong with Bella?'

'I—'

'Tell me, Annis.'

Annis looked again at the photograph.

Bella looked back, all suppressed mischief. Her bare shoulders caught the light. Her mouth was not only trying not to laugh, it had a sensual curve which would raise the blood pressure of any man under ninety. A diamond teardrop, a twenty-first birthday present from her doting stepfather, nestled seductively against her neck under a feathery fall of hair.

Of course there was nothing wrong with Bella. She was blonde, gorgeous and twenty-four. She had a job most people only dreamed about. She was living in the most exciting city in the world. She could have any man she wanted. What could possibly be wrong with Bella?

'No,' said Annis, convinced at last. 'Bella's wonderful.'

She gave Lynda a brilliant smile.

Her stepmother did not respond for a moment.

'Bella would tell you anything,' she said, almost to herself. 'But would you tell me?'

'If I thought there was something really wrong with Bella I would,' Annis assured her. 'But I don't. Honestly. I'm probably just getting myself stewed up about the wedding. You know what I'm like about performing in front of a lot of people.'

Lynda hesitated. But Annis was certain now and it had its effect. Eventually her stepmother nodded, satisfied.

'All the more reason for Bella to be a bridesmaid,' she said practically. 'You know she gets you out of stage fright.'

Annis remembered adolescent drama groups, school concerts, sailing club votes of thanks. Two minutes before she was due to open her mouth, Annis would freeze. That was when Bella would ram a crown down over the brows of one of the peacock boys, or seize a triangle and dodge among the waiting players, refusing to give it back; once she had slid along the polished floor of the church hall on a tea tray and had brought the wrath of a phalanx of church wardens down on her head; once, memorably, she had nearly lost her dress when a shoelace strap had broken at a critical moment. Annis would dive to the rescue. By the time she'd rush out to do her bit on stage, she'd still have half her mind on Bella. None at all was left for her nerves.

'Everyone used to think I was a brilliant speaker and Bella was a tearaway,' she said now, remembering. 'Nobody noticed that the two went together. No tearaway, no speaker—just a frozen jelly with lockjaw.'

Lynda laughed. 'You'd better not get lockjaw at the altar. You get that daughter of mine back, you hear me? You need her.'

Annis did not deny it. She took a decision.

'I'll phone her now,' she said with resolution.

The open-plan office was all limed wood and high-tech silver. No desks. Desks were not chic. The journalists used their laptop computers on tables that were minimalist swirls of wood. Some were shaped like commas, some like 1950's kidney dressing tables. The chairs were somewhere between bar stools and chicken wire. There were lots of mirrors. Every single piece of furniture was on wheels.

'Fluid. Dynamic. We like to keep everything loose,' Rita Caruso, head of features and Bella's boss, had said when she'd introduced her to the room. 'The décor reminds us that the world is in constant flux.'

That had been in November. By Christmas, Bella had been masterminding office-chair races. The course had been three times from glass wall to glass wall ending with a dash round the three central columns and the prize had been an evening clubbing under Bella's direction. Everyone agreed that anyone who went out with Bella was in for a unique experience. As in-house lawyer, Clyde, put it, she was never going to be the queen of cool but by thunder she knew her music. And she could dance. And her contact list was fantastic.

At five o'clock she was sitting at a particularly nasty dagger-shaped desk, trying to talk to a stylist in LA and make notes at the same time without sending all her other notes onto the floor. The silver room was supposed to be a paperless office as well. Background music thrummed through state-of-the-art speakers that looked as if they could make it to the moon under their own steam.

Bella was conscious of pins and needles in her leg, a crick in her neck and fast-evaporating patience with the prima donna on the other side of the country. In fact she was concentrating so hard on not losing her temper that she did not really register the first call.

'Hey, English! I'm talking to you.'

Bella looked round then. Behind her, Sally Kubitchek was waving her hands in the air. Bella put a hand over the little microphone suspended from its twenty-first-century Alice band round her head and mouthed a question.

'Your sister,' yelled Sally.

'Ah.' Bella brought LA back into the conversation. 'Sorry Anton, something's come up. I'll have to call you back.' In the teeth of his protests, she took off her headset and disconnected the cellular phone.

Sally sat in front of a discreet bank of lights. 'Take it in Caruso's room,' she advised. 'She's at the Guggenheim interviewing this month's millionaire. He gave them something amazing and they're showing the press tonight. She won't be back.'

'Right. Thanks.'

Rita Caruso's office had one of the few chairs that was both comfortable and immobile. They all used it when they could. Bella flung herself into its leather embrace as the telephone began to purr sycophantically.

She snatched it up. 'Hi, Annie. How you doing?'

'Hi, Bella Bug. I'm fine. You?'

'I'm cool.'

'How's the job?'

Bella laughed. 'I'm licking them into shape.'

'What?'

'Well, I've had a couple of brushes with the style police but, apart from that, everything's fine.'

'Are you sure?'

'Yup. Caruso says I have a nasty British sense of humour. She likes that. It means I write good copy. I even get to have a crack at interviewing one of her millionaires if I'm a good girl. No, correct that. If I'm a malicious and witty girl.'

'Wow.' Annis was half amused, half shocked. 'I'll buy witty. But you were never malicious.'

'I'm working on it,' said Bella blithely.

She stretched her legs. Her four-inch spike heels just about reached Rita Caruso's desk. She was not a tall girl. But she was going to put her feet on the desk anyway. It was symbolic.

She stretched luxuriously and said, 'So tell me about you. How's the wedding?'

'Growing,' said Annis is a voice of deep gloom.

Bella grinned. 'Told you it would. Quiet wedding isn't in mother's vocabulary.'

'For you maybe.'

It was just as well Annis was on the other side of the Atlantic. Bella's grin did not so much fade as freeze.

Fortunately Annis had no suspicion. 'But I'm not even her daughter,' she complained. 'And I'm too tall for frills and veils. Weddings and I were made for separate universes. But will she listen?'

'No,' supplied Bella. 'The wedding experience pervades every known universe as far as mother is concerned. Even if you bring a sick note, she'll convince herself you want it really.'

She made a huge effort. Her voice didn't sound too bad.

That was New York for you. It taught you to come back with a smart remark even if your heart was breaking. Let's hear it for New York, she thought.

Annis did not detect anything wrong. 'Too right.' She hesitated. 'Er—that's what I was calling about actually.'

Bella's hand was clammy on the receiver. *Please don't ask me to come to the wedding. Please, please, please, Annie.* It was unashamed panic.

'Oh?'

'I need help.'

If Annis had hit her, she could not have winded her more comprehensively.

'Don't ask me,' Bella said, when she got her breath back. She was desperate to keep it at the level of a joke. 'I've never organised a wedding. If you don't trust mother, try one of Kosta's glam friends. There must be a wedding consultant in there somewhere.'

'Probably,' said Annis with the indifference of a woman so utterly sure that she was adored, she hardly noticed the predatory females who still circled round the fashionable architect who loved her. 'But it's not technical advice I want.'

Bella's throat tightened. 'Oh?'

'I want my sister,' said Annis baldly.

For a moment Bella literally could not speak. Everything inside her screamed *No*! Oh, this wasn't fair. This really, really wasn't fair.

'Bella Bug? Are you there? Bella?'

'Yes,' Bella croaked. She cleared her throat. 'I mean, yes, I'm here. Glitch on the line.'

'Well?'

Bella floundered. She felt as if she was drowning.

'Annie, do you know how hard I had to wheel and deal to get this job? American visas are like gold dust. If I go back, I'm not sure they'll let me back in,' she said, improvising desperately. 'Not to work, anyway. I'm here on this six month exchange thing. This is the first proper career-type job I've ever had. I can't afford to risk it.'

The silence was full of disappointment. Bella felt awful but she did not weaken. She could not afford that either. She could feel the tears on her face. She did not know when had she started crying.

This is stupid, she told herself savagely. She did not say anything at all to Annis.

'Oh, well, if you can't, you can't,' Annis said eventually. Her voice was muffled.

She was obviously hurt. Damn! thought Bella. Still, better hurt now than have her wedding day ruined by a sister weeping all over the man she was going to marry.

'Look, I've got to go. There's this guy I need to speak to today. I'll call you and you can fill me in with the news then. Or email me. That's what the Net is for,' said Bella trying to be bracing. Even to her own ears she sounded horridly unfeeling.

'Yes. Of course. I'll call you.'

Annis rang off.

Bella put down the phone and blew her nose hard.

If only Annis had not looked after her from the moment Tony Carew had married Lynda. If only she had not taught Bella how to sail. If only she had not played with her and read to her and let her borrow her make-up. And then, later, if only she had not believed in her when everyone else thought Bella was a pretty airhead.

If only she had not fallen in love with the same man.

But she had. And Kosta Vitale, for all his smooth sophistication, had taken one look at Annis and had fallen right back. Clever, heart-breaking Kosta was undoubtedly right. Annis was a woman men fell in love with. Bella was the girl they took to parties.

But that didn't mean the party girl couldn't fall in love. She just shouldn't expect anyone to take her seriously when she did. And she should get over it as fast as she could.

Well, she was trying. She wasn't doing too badly, either. Sometimes she didn't think of Kosta for a whole hour at a time. Eventually she would get him out of her system altogether. But not if she had to go back to London and watch him walk down the aisle with Annis. Bella knew herself and she knew she was not up to that yet.

She had never told anyone else that she was in love. She had kept her secret well. She had wished them both all the luck in the world and had danced at their engagement party. But Kosta knew she was in love with him. And every time their eyes had met she'd known he knew, even though he'd said nothing. And her heart hurt all over again.

'Love,' said Bella aloud, furiously. 'Who needs it?'

But she would get over it. Of course she would. As long as Annis and Kosta stayed in London and Bella stayed in New York and forgetfulness had time to work its magic.

'Annis, I need you to come with me to New York,' Gilbert de la Court said, without preamble.

Annis was sitting in his office, frowning over a flow chart. She looked up, startled.

'What?'

He gave one of his rare smiles. 'I need camouflage.'

At once she was wary. They had worked together for months and she knew his company inside out but she knew next to nothing about his private life.

But he was thirty-three and single. Good-looking, too, when you got past his complete disengagement from the everyday world. Besides, some women found that air of aloof preoccupation the ultimate sexual challenge. Who knew how many women he was juggling in the few hours he spent away from his computer? Now she came to think of it, just last week he had taken three days off. She was not going to get involved in any domestic battles he might have.

So she said firmly, 'I do management consultancy. You want set-dressing, you go somewhere else.'

He considered that for a moment in silence. Then he said, 'Someone's trying to take over the company.'

His voice was so unemotional, for a moment Annis did not think she had heard him correctly.

He went on levelly, 'That's private. I don't need to tell you that.'

'No,' she said, stunned. 'Do you—I mean—who?'

'An interesting question.' Still no emotion.

Annis thought of the legal structure of the company. She had gone through it with a fine-tooth comb only three months ago.

'They must have someone inside. One of the partners,' she said, thinking aloud.

'Quite.'

Her eyes flew to his face, remorseful. He had three partners, every one of them an old and trusted friend. If this thing was true, then it would be a betrayal of more than business ethics.

'Oh, Gil, I'm so sorry,' said Annis, distressed.

He gave a barely perceptible shrug.

'I can deal with it. I just need to get to New York without arousing the insider's suspicions. I thought—if I said it was part of your analysis of my job but you needed to get it done before your wedding, I would have a sound reason for bringing forward my usual April trip to now.'

'Camouflage,' Annis said, enlightened.

'Yes. Will you do it?'

She hesitated. She had planned to stay in England until the wedding. There was so much to do.

But Bella was in New York. Annis was pretty sure that if she talked to Bella face to face she could get her to change her mind. Maybe even get her to be a bridesmaid. She had not told Lynda yet that Bella had turned her down. Maybe this trip was a golden opportunity.

'Yes,' she said with sudden decisiveness. 'When?'

'This evening.'

Annis gulped.

'I've had Ellen book you a ticket,' he said misunderstanding her reaction. 'All you need is a passport and a toothbrush.'

'And a briefcase if I'm to be any good as camouflage,' said Annis tartly. She was recovering. 'All right. But I'd better get moving.'

She went out to his secretary.

'Ellen, have you really got an air ticket for me?'

His PA grinned. 'And a car booked to take you back to London now and then on to Gatwick airport. And some dollar notes. And your hotel reservation in case you miss the flight. Thinks ahead, does Gil.'

She fished out a package from under her desk.

'High-handed,' said Annis, ruffled.

'I know,' said Ellen, sighing. 'Wasted on a computer, isn't he? Tall, dark and handsome and all he thinks about is Watifdotcom. Never even made it to the Christmas party.'

'Shame,' said Annis absently. She looked at her watch. 'Get that car round and I'll be going. I've got people to talk to if I'm going to be on the plane to New York tonight.'

But she was.

And the next morning, in spite of jet lag and Gil's impassive disapproval, her first call was at the uptown offices of *Elegance Magazine*.

'Annie?' said Bella incredulously on the house phone when the receptionist called up to the office. 'Annie? It's truly you? You're *here*?'

'In person. But I've got a meeting in a couple of hours. Could we have lunch?'

'Sure. I'll just grab my coat. Be down in five minutes.'

It was nearer ten. In that time Bella had the chance to recover from her first surprised delight. She kissed Annis warmly enough but her manner was wary.

Still, she took her by the arm and sped her along the slushy pavements to her favourite Italian restaurant.

'Why didn't you say you were coming when we spoke?' said Bella when they were seated.

'Didn't know. I'm working for one of these do-it-now types. He sprang it on me.'

'Doesn't sound like you to let a man spring something on you.'

'You don't know Gil. He takes single-mindedness to a new plane.'

'Hope it's just single-mindedness about work,' said Bella, trying to tease and, to her own ears, not quite managing it.

Annis didn't hear anything wrong though. She smiled. 'Like I said, you don't know Gil. If he has any feelings, which I doubt, he archived them a long time ago.'

'Sounds a pain.'

'No,' said Annis. 'No, he's not a pain. He's demanding and stimulating and huge fun to work for. He's just single-minded, like I said.'

'Single-minded about what?'

'His work. Computers,' said Annis, conscious of client confidentiality.

'Oh.' Computers bored Bella to tears. 'What we call a dweeb, over here.'

Annis gave a private smile, remembering Ellen. 'His staff don't think so.'

But Bella was not interested in Annis's client. After they'd ordered, she passed her sister under a quick, critical inspection and was pleased.

'You're looking good, Brain Box.'

'Kosta's influence,' said Annis ruefully. 'He's cleared out my wardrobe.'

'And he's obviously taking care of you,' said Bella approvingly.

The pain almost went away when she remembered how happy Kosta Vitale made this dear, difficult sister of hers.

'Yes. He certainly takes care of me.'

When Annis smiled, all the love she felt, all the love she received shone out of her, thought Bella.

'Good.'

'Bella—' But the waiter arrived with their food and whatever Annis was going to say evaporated under a hail of condiments and bottled water and wine.

When he had gone, she said, 'How are you, though? You look very smart. Beautiful as ever.' The 'but' she did not say hung in the air.

Bella knew what she meant.

Only yesterday Bella had gone to the hair salon. Her blonde hair was sculpted into a shining helmet that hugged her elegant head, then feathered out over her shoulders. To the natural gold, Raul had added just a hint of streaking to give it depth and lightness, as he'd assured her. Her legs were still perfect and her figure enough to bring out any red-blooded man in a sweat of lust. But Bella knew, and Annis would see, that she was thinner than she had been. A lot thinner. Her shoulders looked as fragile as bird's bones under the elegant little top. And the moment she stopped talking her face, reflected in the tall mirror behind Annis, was drawn.

'I'm adjusting,' she said carefully. 'It can be a bit stressful.'

'I can see that,' said Annis, equally careful. 'What's your boss like?'

Bella's face suddenly creased into its irresistible gamine grin. 'Impressed. For the first time in her life, apparently.'

Annis grinned back. 'Oh? You must have been writing like an angel.'

'Nothing to do with me. It's all down to you.'

'Explain,' said Annis, entertained.

'Well Caruso never wanted this exchange thing. She doesn't like trainees or foreigners and foreigners begin in New Jersey. But she just loves high-achievers. You and Dad have done it for me.'

'Me?' echoed Annis, genuinely taken aback.

'The consultancy got a name check in the *Wall Street Journal*. Caruso saw it and asked me if that was my sister. So I said yes and basked in your reflected glory.' Bella chuckled at Annis's expression. 'We don't only read about fashion and film stars, you know. Caruso has a regular feature, millionaire of the month. Carry on the way you're going, and I'll get you a slot.'

'Thank you,' said Annis.

Bella laughed aloud.

'No, I haven't got the influence yet. But I'm getting there. Caruso has given me a piece to write about what it's like starting out in New York. It's called New In Town. It's in the April edition. I'll send you a copy.'

'I'll buy it.'

'No need to go that far. I know you never read anything but the financial press.'

'I told you, Kosta's educating me.'

Bella flinched. She could not help it. The name came out of nowhere and she was not ready for it.

Fortunately Annis was concentrating on her fettucini and did not notice.

'I shall expect fan mail, then,' said Bella after a minimal pause. Her amusement did not even sound forced, she congratulated herself.

'Count on it.' Annis stirred her pasta absently. 'Bella, look, I don't want to interfere with your job, of course I don't, but my wedding—'

Bella braced herself. But Annis was talking more to herself than she was to Bella.

'I don't know what's happening. You know that we wanted it to be really small, just immediate family and a couple of friends. But I keep bumping into people who tell me they're coming, though I haven't asked them and neither has Kosta. And we're getting wedding presents from people I haven't seen for twenty years.' Her voice rose. 'Lynda says everything's fine, she's got it all under control, but she doesn't *listen* to me. I don't know what to do.' She looked up then, her face pinched. 'When I said I need you, I wasn't joking.'

Bella stared at her, horrified.

Suddenly she was swamped by memory. Annis was not the cool-suited businesswoman who'd impressed Rita Caruso any more. She was the Annis who had climbed up to get Bella out of the apple tree when she'd been stuck; the Annis who was scared of heights and clumsy with it, but who had still told Bella to stop crying and not look down; the Annis who had got her back on the ground and then had been violently and noisily sick. Anxious and determined and *scared* but still the Annis who did not give up just because she didn't think she could do it.

How could Bella let her down?

Yet how could she not? Surely the best thing for Annis was for Bella to stay away from the man they were both in love with. Annis was going to marry him, after all. Only Bella could not say that she was in love with him, not ever, not out loud. Annis must never know.

'Oh, Annie.' She groaned.

'I mean, if you can't come over until the wedding, that's fine. I can moan to you down the phone. Or email, like you said. Just as long as I know you're part of it. That you'll be there on the day.'

Bella felt as if she were being torn apart.

'I don't know,' she said wretchedly. 'It's so damn complicated…'

'Can we at least talk about it?' said Annis.

'We are talking.'

'I mean properly. Without you looking at your watch every minute. This evening. What are you doing after work?'

Bella pulled a face. 'Taking some honoured visitors on the town. I'm supposed to be the best in the department on the guided tour of the Big Apple.'

'Oh.' Annis was disappointed but not defeated. She fished in her shoulder bag and brought out a typed sheet. 'Let's see.'

She scanned it.

'What is that?' said Bella, recoiling.

'My timetable. My client's idea. When I told him I was coming to see you, he gave me the day's itinerary, so I could catch up with him if I got delayed anywhere.'

Bella was revolted. 'The dweeb,' she said. 'Could he also be a control freak by any chance?'

Her sister smiled. 'He thinks ahead.' She went back to the list. 'Dinner, venture capitalists, blah blah blah. No, that won't do. Hey, what about this? Hombre y Mujer Club, ten-thirty.'

'If you try and talk at Hombre y Mujer you'll get burst eardrums,' said Bella.

'We don't have to talk there. Just meet. Then I could come back to your place and we could thrash this thing through.'

That gives me ten hours to find an excuse she'll believe, thought Bella. Just great.

She said, 'Fine. I'll see you there. Now tell me all the gossip.'

And, recognising that she had won a battle, if not the war, Annis allowed herself to be diverted.

Bella kept the conversation light and away from weddings for the rest of lunch but she knew that the evening was going to be heavy. Everyone noticed how silent she was all afternoon. She still teased the post boy, and was merciless with Sally coming back from a fashion shoot with orange sequins on her cheekbones. But her heart wasn't in it.

'You in love, English?' asked Sally, handing her a revised production schedule.

Bella pulled a face. 'All the time.'

But Sally had a suspicion she wasn't joking.

'Doesn't he like you taking the Japanese on the town tonight? They can get possessive these love-of-your-life types.'

Bella just shook her head and laughed. But Sally noticed in the mirror that as soon as she turned away Bella's laughter died. The only thing that cheered her up, perversely, was a message from her sister that she was feeling too ill to join her at the club, after all. Bella was concerned, of course she was, but Sally saw she was relieved too.

'What's wrong?' she said, calling Annis back at her hotel.

'Something I ate, I expect. Plus jet lag. I'll be better tomorrow. Can we meet tomorrow night?'

'Yeah,' said Bella, resigned. 'Sure.'

But she went to the club anyway. The Japanese had been enthusiastic when offered a Latin beat and Hombre y Mujer was one of the classier venues. It was new, with some great music and a terrific sprung floor. The décor wasn't bad either and the food—if you wanted food—was as hot and spicy as the Cuban beat. A lot of professional dancers went there as well as a lot of Latin Americans. The well-heeled Manhattan crowd had not really found it yet. As a result, said Paco the proprietor, the dancing was as good as you got outside Rio or Havana.

And tonight, thought Bella, she could really dance out her demons. She needed to. She had not felt as desperate as this since the night she never, ever, thought about. The night that had left her with a secret that burned into her soul. A secret she was never going to be able to share. Because Annis was the person she shared her secrets with. Annis was her best friend. And this secret would ensure that friendship ended for ever.

That was why she locked it away. Never looked at it. Went on with her life, just a little damaged, just a little wary. And very, very alone. But alone was all right, Bella told herself. She could handle alone.

So she fluffed out her hair, shook out her shoulders, and sashayed out onto the dance floor.

The hell with tomorrow. Tonight the demons were going back in the box.

CHAPTER TWO

When Gil walked into the club, it was already buzzing. He shouldered his way past the queue and nodded to the bouncer on the door.

'Good evening.' His clipped English accent was very pronounced. 'Paco is expecting me.'

'Oh, yeah. Professor,' said the bouncer, trying the word out as if it was the first time he had said it in his life. 'He said to go on up. First landing, door marked Private.'

He held the heavy door open for him. Gil ran up the stairs.

Paco was in his office, sitting at an impressive desk, for all the world like a captain of industry. But when Gil rapped on the door and pushed it open, Paco leaped to his feet and rushed forward like the enthusiastic freshman he had once been.

'Gil! Great to see you!' Paco embraced him, then held him at arm's length. 'What's with the suit? You look *serious*.'

'And you look like a pirate,' said Gil, taking in the tight black head scarf and a single earring. He was taken aback.

Paco grinned. 'Image. Just like they used to tell us in college. Marketing is everything.'

They went way back, he and Gil. They had met in the days when they'd waited tables and had driven delivery trucks to pay their way through college. Paco had graduated from waiter via barman to nightclub owner and, these days, music entrepreneur.

Gil prowled round the room, inspecting huge signed photographs and a couple of framed disks.

'You've certainly made your MBA pay for itself.'

'You, too, from what I hear.'

Gil swung round neatly. 'What do you hear?' He rapped the words out.

Paco looked surprised at the tone. 'Only what was in the old alumni newsletter. Your company develops cutting-edge research software. That's what it said.' His eyes narrowed. 'Oh, I see. We're talking industrial espionage. That's what you're doing in New York, isn't it?'

Gil flung himself down in a chair. 'Am I that transparent? I must have made it so damned easy—' He broke off. His jaw was as tight as a vice.

Paco looked alarmed. 'Hey, I'm just making social conversation here. What's wrong?'

Gil looked at him for a frowning moment. Then, quite suddenly, he shrugged.

'My famed judgement of people,' he said in a hard voice. 'It's struck again.'

'Ah,' said Paco after the slightest pause.

'Yes,' said Gil, answering his unspoken comment. 'I suppose you thought Rosemary Valieri had taught me all there was to know about duplicitous women? You were wrong.' He sounded savage.

'Oh, it's a woman, is it? The English chick you were supposed to bring tonight?'

'No.' Gil dismissed Annis with a shake of the head. 'My marketing director. The first non-specialist I brought in. She's been with us since the start. I thought she was a friend.'

Paco looked at him with a good deal of sympathy. 'Happens to all of us.'

'We all thought she was a friend. She's betrayed the whole team.'

'Can you sort it?'

'Yes,' said Gil with cold fury. 'I only have to divert my attention from important stuff. Work my butt off getting additional funding. Spend hours with corporate lawyers. Lie.'

Paco was amused. 'That's what makes business a fun world.'

'I trusted her.'

'Big mistake.' Paco gave him a beer. 'But we all do it. Don't beat yourself up.'

'She's got some big investors moving in to take over the company. I only found out who today. And how they're going to do it.'

'Bad. But you're sure you can handle it?'

'Yes,' said Gil. He showed his teeth. 'Oh, yes.'

Paco was briefly sorry for the unknown marketing director. 'If anyone can, you can. You were always the most focused guy in the class. Wish you luck, buddy.' He took a swig of his own beer. 'Now, what do you want to do? Stick around or go back to the hotel to wheel and deal?'

'Wheeling and dealing is tomorrow. Tonight I want to release some major adrenaline.'

Paco was enthusiastic. 'Right on. Have a meal, then boogie. The food's Brazilian tonight. Chef does a mean *feijouada*.'

'Great,' said Gil, getting to his feet.

'We got a great couple of DJs tonight. Real enthusiasts, know what I mean? We've got the PR crowd, too. Some of those kids can really move.' He punched Gil lightly on the shoulder. 'You want to channel aggression, you're in the right place. Let's party!'

They ate the spicy food, talking about old friends and new businesses. It was just like being back in college, Gil thought. The same jokes, the same heady sense they could do anything they wanted if they put their minds to it. All the time, the noise from the dance floor rose steadily.

Eventually Paco pushed back his chair. 'Time I showed myself. Time you hit the floor. Let's prowl.'

On the floor of the club Paco was different, Gil saw with amusement. The homely beer was gone. Instead he strolled around holding a glass of colourless liquid awash with chunks of lime and some anonymous leaves. Gil knew that the leaves were basil and the liquid was mineral water but it looked dangerous.

'Mountebank,' he said affectionately.

'That's what the punters expect,' said Paco. He struck a fencer's attack attitude.

They said in unison, 'Renegade, you will die at the bite of good Corsican steel,' and made a couple of imaginary passes in the air, ending with a high five. Paco looked momentarily startled.

Gil laughed. It seemed like the first time for weeks. He took off his jacket and tossed it behind the bar.

'Enjoy,' said Paco and went to talk to the barman.

Gil strolled round the floor. Paco was right, the dancing was good. The nightclub pulsed with Latin beat. Unbelievably rapid maracas warred with a rock base as physical as a hand closing round the heart. He danced with a dark woman, lithe as a jaguar; then a girl who looked as if she'd just come from the office; a glamorous redhead; a laughing Cuban girl who knew the steps so well she did not have to concentrate and even tried to talk to him a little; another office girl.

And then he saw her. She did not look Latin. She was blonde. Golden hair, luminous skin in the club's hectic lighting. Not tall. Not at all one of the athletic semi-professionals that crowded the floor. But the way she moved—

Gil stopped dead. Something caught in his throat as he watched.

She was dancing alone, quite unselfconscious. Her concentration was total. She moved like a mettlesome horse, graceful yet powerful, and just on the edge of danger. She even stamped like a horse pawing the ground. Gil felt himself break out in a cold sweat.

She was unaware of anyone looking at her. She gave her whole body to the music. Her shoulder-length hair swung from shoulder to naked shoulder. But she did not have the overt sexuality of most of the dancers. Her dancing was spiky, even savage. Was she angry with someone? Maybe herself?

Gil took rapid stock. Paco should know. It was his club. If he was half as good a businessman as he had promised to be, he would know his clientele in depth. Gil eased round the dance floor to the bar where Paco was watching the floor.

'Who is she?' Gil said with an urgent undertone.

Paco did not have to ask. Gil could not take his eyes off her. Neither could plenty of other men. Which, in a lively New York club, was unheard of.

She was light as thistledown. Elusive as quicksilver. Fierce as fire. And oblivious to the hungry stares.

Gil was not oblivious. He saw the stares, recognised the hunger and it infuriated him. More than that, it filled him with a desire to shake the girl awake and make her see what she was doing. So much concentration, so much passion was dangerous. Why couldn't she see that?

Paco looked across at the blonde and pursed his lips.

'She comes with the fashion crowd. New. Been around since Christmas. Don't know her name. Could be a dancer.'

Gil was still watching the vital figure. She was never still, not for a moment.

'She looks like it.' There was a husky note in his voice. The abandoned blonde was magnetic.

Paco raised his eyebrows. 'Want me to ask around?'

Gil smiled. Paco could not quite keep the surprise out of his voice. Gil knew why. Paco knew him very well. He knew that Gil was not into instant lust.

And he wasn't. Not even now, though his pulses were pounding. The girl, writhing and punching the air, was much more than a lust object. She looked difficult. And demanding. A conundrum and a challenge and—

Mine, thought Gil.

He felt exultant yet oddly calm.

'I can find out about her,' offered Paco.

Gil did not take his eyes off the dancer but he reached behind him along the bar and picked up a small bottle of water by touch.

'I think it's time I did that,' he said amused, intent.

He did not even look at Paco before heading out onto the seething dance floor.

Bella was having a wonderful time. She always had a wonderful time. That's what she was known for. The original party girl, ready for anything. She was always laughing. She made everyone else laugh, too. You knew you were going to have a great time when you went out in a group with Bella Carew. Under her lively magic, gloom and despondency turned into star-dust.

Tonight the Japanese fashion editorial team, slowly unbuttoning to the Cuban beat, would have endorsed that enthusiastically. They let their long day of meetings dissolve in the rhythm. Seeing that they were happy, Bella allowed herself to relax. She let the stomping beat take over.

The music changed. One of the boys she had danced with before, caught her by the hand. Matching her steps to his, Bella went into a near perfect copy of the singer's videoed routine. Her partner laughed in delight. She laughed back at him.

I am enjoying myself. That's what I do best.

Except that these days it was getting harder and harder to enjoy herself. Oh, she could stay out late, dancing or talking with her friends. But eventually they wanted to go home. And when Bella got back to her rented loft apartment she was cold. The central heating system was American and efficient. But that had nothing to do with it. This was the cold of loneliness and it bit to the bone. And it was going to be worse tonight, with the prospect of that discussion with Annis tomorrow.

Still, no need to think about that yet. No need to think about that for *hours*. She slid both hands into her hair and swung it, letting her shoulders keep the rhythm as she turned her back to her partner, dancing round him provocatively.

Only to find that someone else responded to the provocation.

The first thing she was aware of was a warm hard hand on the bare skin of her midriff. Bella was so startled she almost missed her step. She looked back over her shoulder at the intruder, indignant.

'Hi,' he said.

Or she supposed that was what he said. It was too loud to hear him and nearly too dark to read his lips. But she could see them with odd vividness in the flickering shadows. Sculpted, sensually full and yet with a tension to them that spoke of deliberate control. A man of passions, then, but passions carefully mastered.

Bella could have laughed aloud at her fantasy. Especially as his mouth was almost all she could see of him.

In the strobe lighting though she could make out that he was tall and thin as a rake. She was aware of deep, intense eyes that seemed to burn into her. And there was a wicked rhythm to his dancing. Behind him, Bella saw her former partner fling up a hand in rueful farewell and move on to one of the other girls without missing a beat.

Which left her hard up against a body that seemed made of steel.

Pliant steel. She gasped, as he flung her away from him, brought her back. While she was still reeling, he clasped her to him in some routine that he was completely master of. Bella did not know it. Between surprise and lack of familiarity with the steps she floundered. For the first time in years she missed her footing several times.

The stranger bent forward, pushing her head back and said in her ear, 'Let me lead.'

It went against the grain because Bella was an excellent dancer, but she did. At once, she seemed to know what he was going to do before he did it. The steel body moulded hers, signed to her what she was to do, and she responded. They were perfect together.

When the track ended, she turned to face him, out of breath and exhilarated.

'Who are you?' they said in unison.

He shook his head. 'You first.'

He offered her the bottle of water. She drank deeply, then tipped some over her hot forehead.

The water dripped down her cheekbones, her throat… She saw him watch a tear-drop slide between her breasts under her scoop-cut top.

He masked it at once but she saw the effect it had on him. It made up a little for being hijacked on the dance floor. She smiled brilliantly at him.

'Tonight I'm Tina the Tango Dancer. You?'

'Tonight?'

She shook her head, so that her hair swung wildly. 'This is New York. You can't expect me to give out my name to anyone who walks up and grabs me.'

He was amused. 'But you look like a girl who likes to live on the edge.'

She winced. That was what everyone thought. Even her family thought Bella could cope with anything. Love them and leave them, that was Bella. Light-hearted. Adventurous. Never, ever, vulnerable.

And she wasn't. *She wasn't.*

That was why she was in this wonderful town alone, putting her life together and telling herself the loneliness would pass as long as she did not let anyone see it.

The disc jockey was talking, promoting his latest mix. Bella tuned it out.

She said airily, 'There are edges and edges.' She passed the bottle back to him. 'You're not telling me your name, I notice.'

'Gil.'

'Just Gil?'

In spite of his amusement, the dark eyes rested on her bare shoulders as if he was hungry. She saw it. A small curl of awareness thrilled through her.

But he answered coolly enough. 'If you're Tina the Tango Dancer, I'm just Gil.'

She liked the hunger. It made her feel alive. Just as the music and the strobe lights and the cold midnight streets outside made her feel alive. As she had forgotten how to feel when she was on her own.

'Fine,' she said, preparing to enjoy herself.

The jockey stopped talking. The unforgiving beat started again. At once Bella was moving: hips, shoulders, feet, all talking back to the music.

Gil, whoever he was, began to dance too. But he made it very clear he was not letting her go. Every time she spun and jumped, his hand was there to guide her back to his side.

Exciting, decided Bella.

She grew bolder, challenging him, trusting him not to let her go. His hands were like iron as she bent away from him, her hair brushing the floor. She straightened, laughing delightedly.

At the end of the set, she was hot and breathless. Gil looked down at her, his eyes glinting. He was not even breathing hard.

He must be very fit.

One of the Japanese visitors came up. Even without his tie, he was still impressively courteous. He made a little breathless bow.

'You have been most kind. We thank you.'

Bella read the signs. 'You're ready to go?'

Mr Ito was regretful. But there was an early plane to catch.

'No problem,' said Bella, detaching herself from Gil and dismissing him from her mind. 'I'll get my coat.'

She was piqued that Gil did not try to stop her. After all that possessive machismo on the dance floor she would have expected him at least to ask for her phone number.

She would not have given it to him. Of course she would not. But he should have *asked*. But when she looked round the tall thin figure was nowhere to be seen.

She shrugged, trying to laugh it off.

In the cloakroom, Rosa, one of the other club regulars, was fluffing out her hair.

'Who's the hunk?' she asked Bella in the mirror.

Bella shrugged again. 'Who knows?'

'Thought you were going for the big one there.'

'Big one?'

'Don't be so prim and English! I thought you were going to let him have a date. For once.'

'You know me. Easy come, easy go.'

'You danced so well together.'

Bella gave her an ironic look. She knew quite well what Rosa was talking about. 'It doesn't always follow.'

Rosa laughed.

Bella retrieved her outdoor things. Her coat was a thick wool mix and ankle length. Her scarf was cashmere and her gloves were lined with mink. New York in February was not kind to bare flesh. She even slipped her strappy sandals into her bag and pulled on fur-lined boots.

Since she was in charge of tonight's official entertainment, she had a limousine on stand-by. She fished her tiny phone out of her recovered shoulder bag and dialled the chauffeur.

'Ready to go Arnie. Back to the hotel. Can you drop me off after? Great.'

Rosa was reapplying lip-gloss.

'Going to see him again?

'He didn't ask.'

'So?' Rosa lowered the lip-gloss and met her eyes in the mirror. 'What's wrong with asking yourself? This is the twenty-first century you know.'

Bella flinched.

'Yeah, so they say. But I've been there, done that and it didn't work.'

'Can't have done it right,' said Rosa with conviction.

Oh, I did it right. He just didn't want me. He wanted my sister.

She said aloud, 'Yes, that must be it.' Her voice was colourless.

'So why not go for the tall guy?'

Because I'm never doing that again, ever.

'Maybe I will. But not tonight. I've got to get the honoured visitors home.'

Rosa accepted that. She was serious about her career too.

'Shame.' She put away her make-up and gave a last encouraging lift to her big hair. 'See you Saturday?'

Saturday was the club's big night. Bella had been a regular ever since she'd arrived in New York.

'Count on it,' she said, throwing off the glooms.

The guests were effusive in their thanks. She stood outside the gleaming modern hotel shaking hands and bowing until she thought her face would freeze. But eventually they went inside and she got thankfully back into the limo.

The driver was looking in his rear mirror. 'Who's the guy?'

'What?'

He jerked his head. 'Just got out of a yellow cab. He's coming over.'

Bella turned to look. A cab pulled away. In its wake it left a figure, just out of the hotel's neon, solitary in the deserted street.

He looks cold, Bella thought, then, involuntarily, *He looks lonely. As lonely as me?*

The man was tall as a tree, a black figure in the blue dark. His shoes were polished, though. She could see the reflection of the hotel's starburst sign skimming across his toes as he moved. It made him look as if he was walking through water.

Like a ghost, or one of the ancient gods, temporarily lost on earth. It was oddly powerful. Bella shivered.

'Don't know him,' she said positively.

But he came over, his heels clipping on the icy pavement. He bent down by her door.

Arnie did not lower the window. He shifted on the seat bracing himself unobtrusively. 'Trouble?' he asked.

Bella was realising that she did recognise the dark figure after all. It was the man who had not asked for her phone number.

'Trouble? I don't think so. He was at the club.'

Gil rapped on the window. Arnie looked across and flicked an experienced eye over him.

'Well, he may be a nut but he's not a bum. That's a thousand-dollar coat. Want to talk to him?'

That dance had been *exciting*. It had made her feel alive. For those hectic minutes in his arms she had even forgotten the soul-killing loneliness.

'Yes,' said Bella.

She got out.

Arnie sat back watchfully. He did not turn off the engine.

Bella huddled her coat around her. She was a New York babe now, meeting sexy strangers with a watchful humour. She gathered her sophistication round her as tightly as the coat.

'This isn't coincidence, right?' Bella said to the tall dark shadow.

Gil nodded. 'Sorry.' He didn't sound it. 'I'm leaving tomorrow.'

'And that's your excuse for following me?'

'Reason. Not excuse.'

'Word games,' said Bella dismissively. She pulled her coat tighter. 'There are laws on stalking you know.' But she sounded more curious than threatening and she knew it.

For a moment he looked completely blank. Then he gave a great shout of laughter.

'I didn't think of that. God, this town is paranoid.'

'It's got nothing to do with this town. I'd say the same in London or Paris.'

'If you think I'm a stalker, why did you get out of the car?' he countered.

It was unanswerable. She stamped her feet, not entirely against the cold, though early morning ice was frosting the kerb. The hotel would send someone out to clear the ice soon, Bella knew.

She said, 'I got out of the car because I didn't want you to make a scene.'

He was unimpressed. 'Why should you care if I make a fool of myself?'

'I care if you make a fool of *me*. I've just delivered some influential people here. I don't want them thinking I'm—' She stopped, realising too late where it was taking her.

'The sort of girl who gets out a car to talk to strangers at two in the morning,' he supplied helpfully.

Bella glared.

He was all innocence. 'What?'

She gave up. 'All right. What do you want?'

'To talk.'

'We talked.'

'No, we didn't,' he said calmly. 'We exchanged pheromones. Very rewarding but now I'd like to go somewhere warm and talk.'

She thought of Rosa's tolerant comments in the cloakroom. Did this man think that they'd danced together so well she would let him take her to bed?

She said furiously, 'No way.'

He blinked. Then, infuriatingly, he gave her a reassuring smile. *Reassuring!* As if she, Bella Carew, sophisticate of three continents, needed reassurance. As if she couldn't handle herself, no matter what a man chose to throw at her.

'I didn't say it had to be private. We can go to an all-night diner somewhere if you want.'

Bella looked up and down the upper east side boulevard with exaggerated irony.

'Oh, sure. You see an all-night diner anywhere?'

'Well, let's go into the hotel. They must have a coffee shop.'

'Oh, great. And my boss's business contacts wander in and see me chatting to this evening's pick up? No, thank you.'

She put a hand on the door handle.

He said urgently, 'Don't go.'

It stilled her. But only for a moment.

Not looking at him, she said, 'You should have asked for my phone number like a normal person.'

He drove one gloved hand hard into the palm of the other. 'I haven't got *time*.'

Bella fumbled in her shoulder bag. The spiky heel of a sandal scratched her wrist. She ignored it and found a business card. Swinging round, she held it out to him.

'Try that.'

He did not take it. He was looking at her very straightly, half impatient, half pleading.

'I mean it. My day is solid with meetings and I have to fly out tomorrow to deal with a crisis at home. I only have tonight.'

It sounded melodramatic in the dark and freezing street. Somehow Bella did not think he was a melodramatic man under normal circumstances. Once again she had the impression of someone utterly alone.

It was a feeling she knew.

She thrust the business card into her coat pocket and said abruptly, 'All right. Arnie will find us a diner. Get in.'

But in fact she gave the chauffeur directions to an all-night café in her own area of the Village. Close enough to run for home if she had to, she thought, defending her decision to herself.

Arnie grunted disapprovingly. But he had been on duty since the morning and he wanted to go home. Bella had persuaded him to a late, late coffee in the past and she knew his habits. Now they had unloaded their guests he would want his bed as much as she wanted not to be alone. He did not protest too hard, and dropped them at the little Italian café two blocks from her building.

Gil Whoever-he-was had the manners as well as the overcoat of a gentleman, Bella found. He held the door to the café open for her. There were a few diners, mostly drivers of delivery trucks in jeans snatching a break before getting back onto the empty early morning roads. Gil led the way past them, then stood until she had seated herself. She slid along the wooden bench against the wall but he did not crowd in beside her. He took a chair on the other side of the table and smiled at the heavy-eyed waitress who joined them.

'What would you like?' he asked Bella. 'Breakfast?'

She shook her head, making a discovery. 'You're English.'

He smiled. 'Don't hold it against me. Coffee? Water?'

It sounded as if he did not realise that she was English too. That pleased her obscurely, and not just because she had been working on her mid-Atlantic accent.

'Gallons of water. And herbal tea.'

'Sure.' The waitress knew her. She was in here often enough between her late night forays with out-of-town business contacts and her early morning runs when she gave up on sleeping. The waitress knew which herbal tea without asking. 'You?'

He picked one of the coffee options at random, not taking his eyes off Bella.

When the waitress had gone he leaned forward.

'OK, Tina the Tango Dancer. Cards on the table.'

For some reason, Bella's stomach felt as if it was in a free-falling lift.

'At last,' she said loudly to disguise it.

'When I saw you in the club, I thought, I know that girl.'

'You don't,' she said positively. 'I'd have remembered.'

He was impatient. 'I know I don't. So would I.'

'You need a better chat-up line,' Bella advised him.

He ignored that, frowning at the salt-cellar. 'I'm not putting this well. Maybe what I meant was, I am going to know this girl.'

He looked up quickly. She did not look away quickly enough. There was a jolt like electricity to an exposed nerve.

'An improvement,' she said flippantly, recovering.

Not fast enough.

'You felt it too,' he said on a note of discovery.

'No, I—'

'Maybe not then. Later. When?' She saw him reviewing their brief acquaintance. 'Outside the hotel. Then. You knew then there was something about me you—recognised.'

Bella shook her head vehemently. She was trying to forget the little moment that had tripped her up when she had thought he was lonely, and in recognising that loneliness had been forced to acknowledge her own.

The waitress brought their drinks. He looked at his double latte as if he had never seen one before.

'It's coffee made with milk,' she said kindly. 'Not as strong as the stuff they put in cappuccino.'

'Don't change the subject. You knew, didn't you?'

The lemon and ginger tea was too hot to drink. Bella refused to meet his eyes and pressed herself back against the wall.

She could not ever remember feeling so out of her depth. She was a seasoned flirt. She was also glamorous and sociable. Men had approached her in every conceivable way. Some had interested her, some hadn't, but she had never felt so uncertain. Her head was whirling and her pulses were thundering as if this was somehow momentous.

As if she was afraid of something in herself. Something completely new.

She said, as much to herself as him, 'All I knew was that you were a great dancer and I love to dance.'

He leaned forward. She could feel him willing her to look up. She could feel the intensity of his gaze on her bent head. It was as physical as if he had touched her.

She said loudly, 'That's all.'

There were a couple of shift workers sitting at a corner table, stocking up on breakfast before they went into work. Bella saw them look across curiously.

They must look completely out of place—Gil in his dark, expensive coat and handmade shoes, she with the remains of her party make-up and a cropped top under her winter-weight coat.

Completely out of place but a matching couple among the truckers and shift workers. It was a long time since she had felt part of a couple.

As if he could read her mind, he smiled.

'No,' he said quite gently. 'That's not all. You know it. I know it. It's bad timing but I know it. No point in lying about it.'

Bella looked at her fingernails. 'I don't believe in bad timing,' she announced. 'There's only bad priorities.'

Gil looked amused. 'You sound like my management consultant.'

Bella flinched. 'My sister is a management consultant,' she said after a moment.

'And you're telling me the consultant's solution would be to change my flight?'

'Maybe. If you've changed your priorities.' She stopped herself abruptly. 'Heck, what do I know? I'm not the brain box of the family.'

His eyes were not only intense, they were very shrewd.

'So what are you in the family? The beauty?'

Bella gave a harsh little laugh. 'You could say so. Much good it's done me.'

His smile was a caress. 'It's pretty damned good for everyone else.'

'Oh.' The compliment took her aback. He had not seemed to be the sort of man to pay compliments. 'Thank you.'

He lifted his cup of coffee, toasting her silently. 'You're gorgeous.'

This time it did not sound so much of a compliment. More a kind of assessment, like her mother taking stock of what she had in her store cupboard.

Bella said slowly, 'You don't sound pleased about it.'

He made an impatient movement. 'Pleased? Hell, no. It's just another added complication.'

Bella stared. 'Complication of what, for heaven's sake?'

'You, me and the advanced class in pair-bonding,' Gil answered literally

'What?'

'Well, we skipped stages two through five right there on the dance floor tonight.'

Bella sat bolt upright.

'No, we didn't. We didn't skip one single stage,' she said outraged. 'Your chat-up technique definitely needs attention.'

'No technique,' he said, spreading his hands eloquently.

'You can say that again,' muttered Bella

'Not when it's important. This isn't a game. And, anyway, I'm not a player,' he added with a grimace. 'Not usually.'

'So what are you?'

He leaned forward, suddenly not laughing at all. 'A man in a hurry.'

Bella met his eyes. She did not want to. But she could not withstand that silent insistence. She saw he meant it.

He took her gloved hand and held it between both of his, as if that would somehow make her understand.

'I can't tell you how awful the timing is. Not just the flight tomorrow—no, today. Everything. I can't tell you how much I've got to clear up before I can even think about dating.'

Bella withdrew her hand. 'You're married,' she said flatly.

That stopped him dead in his tracks. 'What?'

She felt a mild triumph. He was so totally blank. He had not seen that coming. Even now he could not quite believe she had seen through him.

Suddenly Bella began to feel in control again. She almost forgave him his deception. She was still a sophisticate in three continents. Nobody need feel sorry for *her*.

'Your wife doesn't understand you?' she suggested tolerantly. She had heard it before and, oddly, it was one of the things she could deal with, unlike the roller-coaster of uncertainty that Gil Whoever-he-was had put her on up to now. 'The moment you saw me you knew I was the sort of girl who would appreciate how hard you have to work. Or how much you have to travel. Or the time you have to spend with clients.'

He was utterly silenced.

She raised a mocking eyebrow. 'Is that one of the steps you think we skipped at Hombre?'

For the first time he looked at her as if she was a stranger.

'Go out with a lot of married men, do you?' he asked at last, slowly.

'You don't have to go out with them to get to know the spiel.'

His face was unfreezing again. The wide, full-lipped mouth was still eloquent even in the crude neon lighting of the diner. It gave him the brooding mystery of one of the Regency rake poets. And the air of a man who would say any damned thing he liked.

She was still startled when he said coolly, 'Are you naturally cynical? Or has somebody hurt you?'

She jumped as if she had driven a splinter under her fingernail. He watched, interested.

'Still in recovery, are you?'

Bella folded her lips into a thin line to stop them trembling. 'None of your business.'

'Don't worry. You'll get over it. We all do.'

Suddenly she didn't want to talk to him any more. No matter how exciting he was on the dance floor, this was altogether too dangerous to her peace of mind.

She drained her cup and looked at her watch.

He sighed. 'All right. I'm insensitive. Always was. But I'll be sensitive later, when there's time. Tonight—'

'This morning,' corrected Bella with a wide, false smile. 'And late. I really need to get home.'

She stood up.

He said, 'Stay. Just for five minutes.'

But she was not looking at him. Not at the wide dark eyes that could go from melting to mocking with such disconcerting speed. Not at the mobile, expressive mouth. Not at his ungloved hands.

'But we still don't know anything about each other.'

'Oh, I don't know,' she said drily. 'You've taken a few layers of skin off me. How much more do you want?'

She eased out from behind the table and pulled her big shoulder bag in front of her.

'You don't know anything about me.'

'I know as much as I want.'

She held out her hand to him to shake hands and say goodbye. He did not take it.

Instead he got up too and threw some notes down on the table without looking.

'At least let me get you a cab.'

She shook her head. 'Not necessary. I only live a couple of blocks. I can walk. If we see a cab, you'd do much better to take it yourself.'

The sensual mouth set in a stubborn line. 'I'll walk you.'

She shrugged, indifferent. They went out into the street.

'You're not the least bit worried, are you? You think you can handle me,' he said in an odd voice.

Bella huddled her coat up round her ears. She was only too aware that, underneath it, she was wearing silken straps and a bare midriff.

'You're not going to jump on me in the middle of the street. It's too cold.'

'Cold is the ultimate passion killer?'

His breath turned to smoke in the icy air. She was conscious of a sudden flicker of that awareness again. Under her chilly flesh there was warmth and it was turning to him.

She said breathlessly, 'Usually works, yes.'

She was striding out, almost running. To speed up her circulation, she assured herself. Not to get away from the disturbing feeling that if she let him put his arm round her he could keep her safe and warm for ever.

He kept pace with her without effort. She remembered how, in the club, she had had the sensation of extreme fitness. Now it was confirmed. He kept up a steady monologue.

'I'm thirty-three. No wife. No dependants of any kind. I live in Cambridge—that's Cambridge, England—but I travel a lot. I don't like being tied down. And I only do one thing at a time.'

'What do you do?' Bella said, in spite of herself.

He seemed to hesitate. But it was so brief that she could not be sure.

'Research,' he said vaguely. 'I'm a sort of boffin.'

She snorted derisively. 'A boffin with a management consultant on the staff? What do you research into? How to make a million on the Internet?'

He looked annoyed. At least, she was not looking into his face but he *felt* annoyed. His long legs ate up the paving stones until she had to break into a trot to keep up with him.

'You've got a good memory. I barely mentioned my management consultant.'

She was puffing. 'I told you I knew something about you.'

'You told me you knew as much as you wanted to.' He sounded angry and suspicious. 'Was that it? Man with a management consultant must be a good bet?'

Bella was furious. 'What do you think I am, an industrial spy?' she panted.

He stopped suddenly and swung round on her. 'Well?'

She stopped too with relief. She had a stitch. Pride prevented her from putting a hand to it. But not all the pride in the world could stop her grateful in-draught of breath.

'If you remember you were the one who came on to me,' she pointed out when she could speak. 'I've been trying to get rid of you half the evening.'

They were two doors from the brownstone where she had the top-floor apartment.

'And now I'm home. So goodnight.'

She offered an ironic handshake. It did not turn out like that. He took her hand and pulled her towards him.

Bella felt her feet skid on the icy pavement. She fell forward into his arms.

In a second that seemed like a lifetime, she saw his eyes widen. Then narrow…focus on her mouth…grow dark with desire…

Bella found that it was not too cold for a kiss. A kiss so passionate that it seemed to light up the sky. A kiss so intimate that it set her blood humming, reminding her that under the coat she was nearly naked. A kiss so new that it left her shaken and silenced when he put her away from him.

It seemed to have shaken him too. He looked down at her, unsmiling.

Under his breath he said, 'This is crazy.'

'Yes,' said Bella, stunned.

He looked at the stone steps to her front door. 'Let me come up.'

She nearly did. So nearly. And not because she did not want to be alone in the cold blue morning.

But then she looked at that curly rakish mouth and got a grip.

'Oh, you can't risk me prising any more of your secrets out of you,' she said nastily.

And ran away from him, her feet slipping every which way on the icy surface. Bella did not care. She had her key out as she ran up the steps. She did not know if he tried to follow her. But she closed the door and leaned against it with her heart hammering.

'The sooner he gets on that damned flight of his the better,' she muttered.

She ran all the way up the stairs to her flat as if he was watching her and it was a point of honour not to stop and look back.

CHAPTER THREE

IT WAS an interesting night.

For weeks, months, every time Bella had closed her eyes, she had seen nothing but her own horrible mistakes. This time there was someone else in her head. Well, he was so insistent, he might as well have been in her head. Everything he'd said echoed.

'You look like a girl who likes to live on the edge.'

What made him say that? Was it true?

'We exchanged pheromones.'

'Oh we did,' said Bella into the privacy of her mangled pillows. She would never have admitted it to anyone else. She shivered and pulled the duvet up to her chin.

'You felt it too.'

She sat up and the duvet fell. 'No I didn't,' she said loudly.

'Let me come up.'

And if she had?

This is crazy, she told herself. *Too much emotion followed by too much salsa. I have never reacted to a man like that in my life. It isn't even as if I'm looking for a relationship. I know I've got to get over Kosta before I can do that. If I ever do.*

So what on earth is going on?

She could not answer that. She tried, for hours it seemed. At six-thirty she gave up. The sky was still dark but the midnight blackness had gone.

Traffic started to rumble. The undefeated birds who stuck it out through the New York winter started to twitter. Bella usually left crumbs and water for them on the fire escape. Every morning she went out and broke the ice in the bowl.

Reminded now, she untangled herself from the covers. She pulled on track-suit bottoms, Aran sweater, gloves, and woolly hat and began to struggle with the dead-bolts.

'Let me come up.'

She had not let any man into this eyrie of hers. Privacy might be painful but it was precious. Until now she had not been tempted. Why had Gil Whoever-he-was been the first to offer that dark temptation?

The trouble was, that bit was easy. He was gorgeous. All that dark intensity. The way he moved. The way he kissed.

Forget the way he kissed, Bella advised herself dourly. *He's leaving New York and just as well. How many complications do you want in your life at one time?*

She got the door open. The small birds retreated to a neighbour's guttering and sat there, lined up like a border patrol, watching her. She picked up the stick she kept for the purpose and smashed the ice. It was thinner than it had been last week. So there was no accounting for the violence with which she went at it. Bella shivered, put the stick down and clapped her gloved hands together.

What was it about him?

All right, he was a good dancer. So were half the men in New York. Anyway, she couldn't let a man get under her guard just because he knew how to slide his hips round hers. It was crazy. Even in her former days of extreme party-going, she had never lost sleep over a guy she had danced with once.

The birds watched her. She fetched the wild birdseed she had bought to augment her stale bread and scattered it. A lot missed the old plate she had designated as a bird feeder and fell through the ironwork. A few of the braver birds left their guttering and started picking among the seeds four floors below.

The little flock pushed and jostled and flew at each other. They looked like children in a playground before school. Small struggles but basically companionable. Bella smiled, remembering how she'd set up a skipping game she had learned on the street when she'd gone to the first smart school that her stepfather, Tony, had sent her to. She had not done too badly at fitting into the new rich crowd. She was not doing too badly at fitting in here either, come to that. It was just—

The cold of exile struck suddenly, as it always did. It was shocking as a knife slash. Bella bit her cold lip until it bled.

But it was her own fault. She need not have been alone this morning.

'Let me come up.'

Her blood still hummed, like the crazy moment when she so nearly had done just that.

Yet, if she had, she would still have been alone this morning, Bella thought. Even if he was still here, she would have been alone. She had been alone ever since Annis and Kosta fell in love. And she started to pretend.

I'll be pretending for the rest of my life, she thought desolately.

Bella was shivering badly. She went back inside and flung the bolts into place.

But she did not want to go back to the rumpled, lonely bed. Instead she made herself some coffee and sat at the breakfast bar. She had flung her notebooks down there yesterday. Now she pulled them towards her, starting to rough out another of her New in Town columns. Rita Caruso had not commissioned it but what the heck? If she had a piece ready and they had a slot to fill, it might come in handy. At least it took her mind off the irresolvable dilemma of what on earth was going on last night.

Gil had a breakfast meeting with the patent lawyers. He had never found it so difficult to concentrate.

He should have tried harder. On the other hand, maybe he should not have come on so strong. At least he should have taken her business card when she'd offered it to him. How could he have let her walk away from him like that?

When the senior lawyer started to explain the evolution of intellectual property law, he nearly lost it. A figure like a flame danced just out of vision. He knew it was only in his imagination but his body responded as if she were in the room.

Get a grip, he thought, between shock and amusement. *There are a lot of people depending on you here. Tina the Tango Dancer is strictly an after-hours activity.*

'I'm sorry,' he said to the lawyer. 'I don't think I quite understood that. Could you run it by me again?'

She didn't invade the corporate lawyers' meeting because he kept asking questions. Gil always found it was a useful discipline. But he had never needed it so badly before.

He took Annis with him to meet the bankers. He was going to use some of her work, after all.

In the cab she said, 'Are you all right?'

It startled him. 'Sure. Why?'

'You look different,' she said doubtfully.

He was not surprised. He felt different. He had never felt so alive.

Tina the Tango Dancer, I'm going to find you again, he promised silently.

Aloud he said, 'This is all new for me.'

'Me too,' said Annis. She gave him an encouraging smile but she was looking wan this morning too. He said so.

'Things didn't go as well with my sister as I hoped,' she admitted. 'We're going to talk it over again this evening. But, frankly, I'm not hopeful. Bella is the loveliest person. But when she makes her mind up—' She sighed. 'Oh, well, no point in thinking about that yet. Tell me how you want to play this meeting.'

Gil excised the mocking blonde ghost. This meeting was a matter of survival. He would concentrate on his private life once he had secured the future for the people who were dependent on him. For the moment, he had another priority.

An hour later he looked round the faces at the shiny boardroom table and drew a long breath.

Well, I've given it my best shot. If they don't buy that, goodbye independence.

He did not let it show of course. After the crash course Annis had given him in the ways of high-management skills and even higher finance, he sometimes thought his face had frozen. It was still the same face when he looked in the mirror: high cheekbones; aquiline nose; gold-flecked brown eyes that his female students used to say were melting. And then that problem mouth. Not just his students, every woman he met took one look at his mouth and decided he was an unbridled voluptuary. It had taken professional advice to tell him that. It had taken a lot more than advice to curb its effect.

Even after months of practice, Gil knew he could not afford to relax his guard for a moment. He needed these bankers to think of him as a keen businessman, not a dreamer. And certainly not a sex object. So he schooled his features into arctic aloofness and tried to forget that he had ever had any spontaneous feelings at all.

Or that every single spontaneous feeling had been aroused only a few short hours ago. *Tina, you have a lot to answer for*, he told the mocking phantom, with a silent groan.

'You're very sure about this,' said one woman. 'Why?'

He could answer that without thinking. 'Because I needed it. I designed this system because I wanted to do all those things. There just wasn't a package I could buy that gave it to me.'

'Not a single package maybe.' That was the industry specialist. Gil had been at MIT with him. 'But surely if you went looking, bought a number and spliced them…'

'No,' said Gil. 'I tried that.' He looked round the table. 'Believe me, I never set out to design a system. I was a user of this stuff. And there's nothing out there that will give me what this new system of mine will give. Watifdotcom lets anyone buy some time on the system to do their own research.'

They all looked intrigued. Gil forgot that they were New York bankers. They were people who wanted to understand something that puzzled them. Just like his students. Just like his small staff. And he was good at explaining.

His laptop computer was still connected to the screen at the end of the room. He cleared the page of projected sales.

'Look,' he said, typing furiously. Icons began to burst onto the screen. 'Here you have the information sources. Almost infinite. And here you have the possible functions. Too many to count easily.'

He leaped up and went to stand beside the screen at the end of the room. He felt comfortable at once. This was what he knew. He could run a class with nothing but a blackboard and his enthusiasm and he always had. Underneath, these guys wanted what he had: a vision.

They were all looking at him expectantly. Gil grinned, suddenly sure he was going to bring this off.

'You want to do something original? OK, you need to control your material, you've got to have choice.' He stabbed one of the icons on the screen before looking back at them. 'But you also need an element of surprise. The random attraction that pulls you off any path you could have forecast.' He flung his arms out. 'And, hey, welcome to a new universe. This is the way it works…'

Afterwards he was not so sure it had been a good idea to turn the meeting into a seminar. He got his face back under control but something told him that the whole atmosphere had changed.

Not that he could tell it from the way they looked at him. They all wore impassive expressions to rival his own, at least when he was remembering. Six months ago, Gil would have despaired. For a moment he nearly did.

But his friendly consultant, currently sitting composedly beside him with her neat hands in her lap, had insisted he read up on body language. He had and, like everything Gil did, he had had done it thoroughly. In meetings these days even his handshake was carefully calculated.

So he knew what to look for. Finger-tapping, shoulders turned away from him, disengaged eye contact—they would all be bad signs. There were none of them! Everyone round the table was still looking at him.

Inspired, he added, with that upper-class English diffidence they all liked so much, 'It's a neat little system. We're all rather keen on it.'

The hard woman at the head of the table laughed. It was a friendly laugh.

For the first time in the last horrible days, Gil began to let himself hope. Really hope.

Tina, you brought me luck, he told his unseen companion.

Back in control, he did not let it show.

'I agree. It would be a real shame to sell that to a bunch of asset-strippers. You want it to stay in the hands of people who will push it to its full potential,' said the industry specialist.

'You're a believer, Mick,' said the hard woman. But she said it tolerantly. 'OK, Professor de la Court. You've convinced me I'm looking at the twenty-second century here. Now convince me there are enough future techno-freaks out there to buy into it today.'

Gil did.

The sales statistics did not excite him like the WATIF system did but he knew them backwards. It took a surprisingly short time. The bankers asked fewer questions than he had expected. He and Annis had foreseen all of them. He answered without hesitating.

'OK. That wraps it up for me,' said the chair briskly. 'Anybody else?'

The team shook their heads.

'Then, thank you, Professor de la Court, Ms Carew. We'll get back to you.'

Outside the bank Gil said, 'I've got something I need to see to. See you back at the hotel?'

'I'm seeing my sister before the flight,' Annis said warningly.

'Oh. Well, I'll see you on the plane anyway. Best to make our own way to the airport?'

'Sure.'

He raised an arm to call a cab.

Something in his face made Annis say, 'What are you up to, Gil?'

He looked down at her, amused. 'Why do you ask?'

'Because I'd have thought that fighting for your commercial life was pretty exciting. But you haven't lit up like this until now.'

His eyes danced. 'Ah, but this one is a real challenge.'

Annis cast her eyes to heaven. 'Don't tell me. You met some computer genius at that club of yours last night. You're recruiting again.'

He laughed out loud at that. 'Wait and see,' he said aggravatingly.

And jumped into a yellow taxi that skidded to a halt in front of them.

Annis stamped her feet on the ice-dusted pavement, puffed out her cheeks and turned her steps to the hotel.

Gil did not have much luck at the blonde's apartment house. A woman with half-moon glasses and a suspicious nature refused to tell him so much as the girl's name. There were six names to choose from and nothing to show the sex or marital status of any of them. None of the initials was T.

So she was not called Tina. Well, he had not really thought she was. He retired to the diner where they had had coffee but no one there seemed to know her either. Or if they did, they weren't admitting it.

In fact they were not really interested in him at all. One of the waitresses had a long-stemmed rose tucked in her waistband and both of them were exclaiming over a Cellophane-wrapped bouquet that a trucker had brought.

'Somebody's birthday?' said Gil, trying to ease his way into their good graces with friendly chat.

The girls looked at him with scorn. 'It's Valentine's Day.' They did not actually add 'dummy' but it was there in their tone.

'Valentine's Day,' said Gil on a long note of revelation. 'Valentine's Day. Just what I need.'

Bella got to work early after her disturbed night. No one in the office noticed. They were all too busy with the next issue. And then, when they had finally concluded their editorial meeting, the big glass-walled room was full of cries of well-simulated surprise as baskets of flowers arrived hourly.

'Oh, look at those,' said Sally, as a tall basket-weave horn of crimson roses was winched onto the circular table at which Bella was working today. 'Someone loves you.'

'Not me,' said Bella cheerfully. 'These are for Rita.'

'Don't believe it. None of her men survives long enough to send flowers,' said Sally positively.

Bella laughed. 'Then, the undead are doing great. She's got four major arrangements in there already and the day is young.'

Sally shook her head disapprovingly. 'Then, freeze onto the roses. You don't want to be the only woman in the place without a Valentine bouquet.'

'I didn't know it was competitive.'

'That's because you've never worked in an office before. Of course it's competitive.'

Sally's own desk bore a very pretty posy of primroses and violets. It had come with a card she was not showing anyone. But every time she took it out and read it—which was at five minute intervals—she blushed.

It was that, rather than Rita Caruso's lustrously blooming office, which made Bella feel restless.

'I don't think we take it so seriously in England.'

Sally popped her eyes. 'No roses? No romantic gestures?'

'I've had cards but they are usually jokes,' Bella admitted.

Sally muttered darkly about the stupidity, crassness and general lack of imagination on the part of Englishmen.

But Bella did not want to think about Englishmen. They had a habit of whispering 'Let me come up' in her ear when she ought to have been concentrating on work or screwing her courage to the sticking point to go to the wedding.

She said hastily, 'Maybe it's me. After all, none of the New York guys are sending me flowers either.'

'Only because you never let them get beyond the first date. Even so, I wouldn't be surprised if the guy from finance—'

'I don't think so.'

'Why not? If even Caruso gets roses, when people know she eats a new man every time there's a full moon, you've got to be in with a chance.'

'Rita has column power. I'm not doing a feature on anyone.'

'So young. So cynical,' mourned Sally. She grinned suddenly. 'You're learning, English.'

Bella laughed. But, even so, being the only woman to leave the office without flowers was surprisingly uncomfortable. Swaying on the overcrowded subway to meet Annis, she assured herself that she was glad not to have to be struggling with a bouquet. But the habitual winter public transport smell of wet raincoat and cough syrup was shot through with the scent of hot-house flowers.

Annis was waiting for her in the lobby of the hotel with her overnight bag.

'Coming to stay?' said Bella, surprised.

'I'll go straight on to the airport from wherever we eat. That gives us a good long evening. I've only got carry-on luggage, so I don't have to check in till the last moment.'

'Great,' said Bella hollowly.

But it was not Annis who brought up the subject of the wedding.

'I thought you guys were determined to keep it small,' said Bella, as they were talking about Lynda. 'How can you have let Mother get so out of hand?'

Annis was philosophical. 'You've got to be realistic. Tony is rich and noisy. And Kosta…' her eyes lit with remembered warmth '…has his following on the social circuit.'

Bella smiled. It was an effort but it had to be done. She could not pretend Kosta did not exist. Annis might suspect something.

So she said truthfully, 'Of course he has. He's very tasty. Half of London will go into mourning when he takes himself out of circulation.'

Annis regarded her with something bordering on exasperation. 'You are so right. Think about it.'

Since Bella had been working hard at blanking out the wedding altogether, this was not advice she welcomed. It was one thing to know that Annis and Kosta were happy, half the world away. It was quite another to go and watch them snuff out all her dreams.

'What?'

'Half of London will be thumbing through the photographs seeing who isn't there. You know as well as I do that the papers are going to pick it up, no matter how quiet and countrified we try to keep it. What are they going to say about the absentee sister?'

Bella had not thought of that. Annis was right. There had to be at least a chance that some unfriendly gossip columnist would suggest that the bride's sister was too jealous to come. And from there it was a short step to speculating *why*. It was an unwelcome thought. She had kept her secret so far. She did not want a journalist with a few hours to spare digging it up and printing it.

'You can keep the press out if you want to,' she muttered.

'We can try. I wouldn't bet much on our chances.' Annis paused. 'Anyway, it's not just about the press, is it?'

'I thought you said—'

'Oh, Bella, we're sisters. I want you at my wedding.'

Bella gritted her teeth until her jaw hurt.

'Yes, I know,' she said at last in low voice. 'I always thought I'd be there right behind you, holding your flowers and making sure you didn't bolt.'

Annis gave a rather watery laugh. 'Well, then—'

Briefly Bella wondered if hiding her feelings had been the best course of action. Maybe it would be healthier for everyone if she made a clean breast of it now?

Annis saw her hesitation and misinterpreted it. She said quietly, 'If you don't come, it will always be there, in the family album, for ever. The Bella-shaped gap.' She looked at her sister, torn between affection and despair.

'Please?' said Annis.

What could Bella do?

'I'll think about it.'

'I didn't broach it before, but you know what ought to happen. You want to be a bridesmaid. I want you to be a bridesmaid. What is important enough to get in the way of that?'

'I know,' Bella agreed, wretched. And because, in spite of her broken heart, Annis was still her best friend, she gave her a hug and said, 'Let's go eat and I'll give you my New York update. Next time you *will* stay with me. We'll order in and it will be like it used to be. Oh, it's good to see you.'

And it was. It really was. By the time Annis called a cab to take her back to the airport, they were giggling like schoolgirls. It was almost as if they had never been apart.

It stayed with her as she sat on the subway, too preoccupied for once to eavesdrop on her fellow passengers. It even stayed with her as she trudged through the icy slush to her building. This could not be the end to all those years of friendship.

'Hi, Bella,' said a voice above her head.

She jumped and skidded, nearly falling on the slippery pavement. She looked round wildly.

Mrs Portnoy from next door was hanging out of her window. Bella stared up, open-mouthed. No one hung out of their windows in weather like this.

'I was looking out for you,' said Mrs Portnoy in explanation. 'Took in a delivery for you. I think. You'd better come up.'

Mrs Portnoy was the Mrs Fixit of the neighbourhood. She was also an incorrigible gossip.

Bella hid her reluctance. Mrs Portnoy had introduced her to the best delicatessen in town. 'OK.'

'Come up.'

Mrs Portnoy closed the window.

Bella trod up the steps of the brownstone next door. Half an hour, she promised herself.

Mrs Portnoy was excited. She pulled her inside.

'So romantic. He looked real handsome too. Course I didn't tell him anything about you. He said he only saw you the once. It's like a movie.'

Bella was aware of strong sense of foreboding. 'What is?'

Mrs Portnoy led the way into a parlour stuffed full of furniture that had not been changed since 1950. She talked all the time.

'He must have chosen every bloom personally.'

Suspicion began to crystallise. 'Who did?'

'See for yourself.'

Mrs Portnoy stood back with a large gesture.' The flowers deserved it.

Bella stared. She had never seen such an enormous bouquet in her life. Or such a red one.

She could well believe that her unknown admirer had chosen every flower himself. No professional florist would have put together such a collection of scarlets and crimsons and orange. Any shade that technically fell into the red sector of the spectrum was represented. Blood-red. Wine-red. Brick-red. Rust and rose and ruby. Whoever he was, he was not a moderate man. Not the sort to send a dozen roses and think he had made his point. Her blood began to tingle at the thought.

'Wow. That hurts,' said Bella involuntarily.

What had Sally said? Englishmen had no imagination?

Mrs Portnoy grinned. 'Guess he thinks it's your favourite colour.'

Bella did not ask who. She did not need to.

Mrs Portnoy held out a piece of paper. It was a page off a roll of paper for a portable printer. The perforated borders were still attached.

Bella did not recognise the address or the signature. But she recognised the name on the top all right.

To Tina the Tango Dancer,
Happy Valentine. We will salsa again soon. If I don't catch up with you tonight, call me. Call me anyway.

There followed a whole raft of numbers and email addresses. He was Gil@dcourt.com. But he had not bothered to sign his full name to it—

or remind her when and where they had met. Of course he had not needed to. But he did not know that. Or he shouldn't have known it, thought Bella, fulminating.

'Coffee?' said Mrs Portnoy, scenting intrigue.

'Thank you,' said Bella. Now that she had got over the strange, tingling feeling, her resolution to get out fast was forgotten in sheer fury.

How dared he send her that imperious message and not even bother to sign it? Oh, how dared he? And those flowers! They were a message all on their own.

'You like red?' said Mrs Portnoy, returning with coffee and spiced biscuits.

'Hate it,' snapped Bella.

Mrs Portnoy blinked. Bella was remorseful. She reminded herself that it was not Mrs Portnoy's fault that she was Gil's messenger in this.

'He said he'd been to the flower market,' Mrs Portnoy told her in congratulatory tones.

'Very focused,' said Bella between her teeth.

The unwelcome voice in her head said, *'I only do one thing at a time.'*

And one colour by the look of it.

'They make my eyes sore.'

Mrs Portnoy sighed with pleasure. 'The colour of love. The colour of passion. I remember when I was your age, my Sam…'

For once Bella was grateful for the legacy of legend left by the late Samuel Portnoy.

Love, she thought. *Passion, for heaven's sake. One dance, two conversations and a kiss doesn't add up to passion.*

But that didn't allow for the quality of the kiss. Even now, hours later, she shivered with reaction when she recalled the sudden total physical awareness—of him, of herself. Of the cold night. Of the quick blood in her veins. Of his warm flesh and hers and the ease with which they could have gotten rid of the layers of clothing between.

Was that a sort of passion?

If it was, thought Bella, she did not want to have anything to do with it. She had listened to her instincts when she'd fallen for Kosta Vitale. Look where it had left her! Half the world away from her family and friends trying to screw up her courage to go home for the shortest possible visit to her sister's wedding.

No, no more listening to her instincts for Bella Carew. She was going to take charge of her feelings. Passionate kisses were fine and fun but they were no signpost to the future. And the future was what she had to concentrate on if she was ever going to get out of this messy misery. What she needed was less agonising over her instincts and a good solid injection of self-respect.

That was when Bella made up her mind about three things: she would do the full bridesmaid performance and face it out; she would never call a man who did not give her his full name; and she was taking that bouquet to work tomorrow.

She did just that.

Sally was impressed. Even Rita Caruso was impressed.

'Secret admirer?' she said thoughtfully. 'Maybe you could get an article out of that. As long as he's not a stalker, of course.'

'Not that secret,' said Bella drily. 'And speaking of articles—'

She whipped out her offering on Latin life that described her evening at Hombre y Mujer. Well, part of her evening.

Rita Caruso took it away to think about.

It was the start of a hectic time. Caruso liked her writing but, she pointed out, Bella was supposed to be on a training programme. So she had to do all the dogsbody's duties before she was allowed to write.

So Bella did. She ran around at fashion shoots, she sent flowers to celebrities, she took notes.

In her private life she sent Annis her measurements for the bridesmaid's dress and then resolutely put the wedding out of her mind. Instead, she shopped. She hung out with the girls. She helped build a snowman in Central Park and then joined in the snowball fight afterwards with ferocious accuracy. She got column inches out of all of them. She laughed all the time and there were only two things her friends found she wouldn't do.

She would not go anywhere near Hombre y Mujer.

And she wouldn't say who had sent her the flowers.

CHAPTER FOUR

BELLA tried to put Gil out of her mind. She really tried.

He did not try to get in touch with her again and she told herself she was glad. Of course she was. His flowers had died and so, she assured herself, would the unsettling echo that haunted her dreams. If she concentrated.

Heaven knew she had plenty to do. Rita Caruso agreed to give her enough unpaid holiday to go home for the wedding but, in return, she piled tasks on her until Bella's desk became a sea of paper. Caruso beamed and promised her a three-thousand word article.

'Like I need more work.' Bella groaned.

'Like you need a bodyguard,' said Sally without sympathy. 'Do you know how many staffers are after that slot?'

When she did, finally, get out of the office, life was just as hectic. She had to get new clothes, to show everyone what a fabulous time she was having in New York. And her air ticket. And a wedding present, though that was almost impossible.

What did she buy for the love of her life when he was marrying someone else? What did she buy her sister when she was walking down the aisle with her only hope of happiness? And she knew she'd helped them do it?

So, between all her tasks, she managed not to think about the maddeningly silent Gil Whoever-he-was more than three or four times a day.

By the time she got back to London just days before the wedding, she had almost buried him.

Almost.

She was going to see Annis at once. Her plane touched down at ten in the morning but knew the meeting could not be put off. She only had a carry-on bag so she did not have to wait for baggage to be unloaded. She felt oddly shaky, as if she was going to see a hostile stranger instead of a stepsister who was her best friend.

Maybe the problem was in going to Annis's flat—Annis ran her consultancy from home—and in coming face to face with the major changes in Annis's life since the last time Bella had been there. At this hour, Kosta would have gone to work, of course, so she would not have to see him yet. But there would still be his things around. There had to be.

'I can bear it,' said Bella between her teeth. 'This is stupid. Of course I can bear it.'

But her stomach still churned as she walked out of Terminal Three and joined the queue for black taxis.

The one she got was furnished with a telephone. She used it to call Annis.

'The plane was early. Is it still all right if I come straight to you?'

'Surely.' Annis had a lovely voice, warm and full of laughter. Her affection, reaching out across the crackling reception, did a lot to soothe the turbulence in Bella's digestion.

'A client has dropped by—' although Annis valued her privacy, sometimes a client who became a friend was asked into the pretty flat '—but we'll be finished by the time you get here.'

'Are you sure?'

'Absolutely. Hurry along Bella Bug. I'm putting the coffee on now.'

The nervous acidity subsided altogether.

'I've missed you,' Bella said involuntarily.

'Me too. Can't wait to see you.'

Annis rang off. Bella sank back on the seat, blinking away tears but smiling.

When she got to the luxury block of flats, she almost danced through the foyer. She nodded to the porter. He knew her well. Up to four months ago, he had seen her several times a week.

She hummed going up in the lift. When Annis threw open the door, Bella flung her arms round her with a shout of glee.

'Oh, it's so good to be home. I missed you so much. You look wonderful. Tell me—'

The words died in her throat.

Standing behind Annis, his face unreadable, was a man whose kiss she had put so much effort into forgetting.

Bella dropped her arms and her overnight bag and let out a wail of pure panic.

'Oh, *no*!'

Annis did not understand, of course. She was evidently taken aback.

She cast a quick, bewildered look at her visitor before saying, 'It's all right. You haven't interrupted a meeting. Gil was just going.'

Gil. He wasn't taken aback at all. Bella met his eyes.

He was expecting me, she thought, suddenly certain. How long has he known who I am? Her jaw tightened.

Annis said uncertainly, 'Bella?'

Bella swallowed. 'Right. Er—sorry.'

She did not know what she was apologising for but it filled up the horrible silence while he looked at her without speaking. Which was just as well, as she was hearing his voice rather too clearly in her head. It was not saying anything she would want Annis to overhear.

Bella fumbled for her bag. Her hands felt crazily weak. She looked anywhere but at him as she hauled the strap of her overnight bag over her shoulder.

At last he spoke. 'Gil de la Court.' He held out his hand.

Bella did not move. She knew that voice all right. It had shared her pillow more often than she wanted to remember. She stared at his hand, mesmerised.

More and more bewildered, Annis said, 'My sister, Isabella Carew.'

'Nice to meet you,' said the voice in a neutral tone.

But it was still the voice that had been whispering in her ear every night for what seemed like a lifetime, *'You felt it too.'* Bella felt as if she were in a nightmare.

He found her hand somehow, pumped it briskly up and down a couple of times and dropped it, turning back to Annis.

'I'll call you when I've heard what the bankers have to say.'

Annis was taking Bella's bag from her and drawing her inside.

'Great. We can get together afterwards, if you like.'

'Really?' He looked sceptical.

Annis chuckled. 'I'm not getting married until Saturday, Gil. Up to then I'm all yours.'

Bella flinched. Annis looked down at her in surprised concern.

Gil de la Court did not look surprised at all. 'Miss Carew thinks you should be concentrating on pre-wedding girl talk.'

'No way. I want a career to come back to,' said Annis with feeling. 'Good luck with the bankers. Catch you later.'

'Goodbye, Annis.' He nodded to Bella, expressionless. More than that—indifferent. 'Nice to meet you.'

Indifferent? How could he be indifferent?

You sent me flowers. All that hot red, the colour of passion. You called me Tina the Tango Dancer. You wanted to spend the night with me.

She wanted to scream it at him.

Of course, she didn't.

She knew why he was indifferent. That was then, and this was now. Then she was a wild child with a salsa addiction. Now she was his management consultant's sister with jet lag and a five-hour time change on the clock.

'Goodbye,' she said colourlessly

Annis closed the door on him and looked into Bella's pale face.

'Jet lag?'

Bella seized the excuse gratefully.

'I was working late last night. Went straight from the office to the airport.'

Annis raised an eyebrow. This did not sound like Bella.

'Interesting job?'

Bella laughed. Some of the colour was coming back into her face.

'Necessity. I haven't really worked there long enough to be entitled to a holiday. I only blagged a few days out of them because my boss is sentimental about weddings. She also thinks I might come back with some tasty copy on the English society wedding.'

Annis led the way into the kitchen where a coffee pot was bubbling in welcome.

'You'll have to make it up, then,' she said. 'This is strictly family and friends. Not an English society in sight.'

'That's a relief.'

Annis put her arm round Bella's waist and squeezed. 'Oh, it's so great to have you here. I have a nasty feeling I'm going to be horribly scared walking down that aisle.'

'You mean you want me there to block your escape route?' Bella teased her.

Annis poured coffee. 'Maybe.'

Bella took the mug gratefully and warmed her hands round it. Her hands were still icy, in spite of the central heating. Residual shock, she supposed. Just walking into him like that—

She brought her wandering thoughts back ruthlessly. 'You haven't really got cold feet have you?'

Annis propped herself against the refrigerator and swirled her own coffee. 'No, but—it's a big step.'

'You're good at big steps,' Bella said bracingly. 'Look at the way you set up your own business. No help from Dad.'

'This is different.'

'Yeah, sure.'

'It is.' Annis looked up quickly. She looked troubled. 'I knew I could run the business. It's what I'm good at. I'm not good at—' She stopped.

Bella did not pretend to misunderstand. 'This is about men, right? OK, you made your mistakes. So does everyone.'

Annis shook her head. 'That's too easy. *You* never messed up like I did. No live-ins who walked out, shouting. When you said goodbye to a man you stayed friends.'

'Maybe that's because neither of us was that involved in the first place,' Bella said lightly, though it hurt. 'You know me and men, Brain Box. Easy come, easy go.'

Certainly nobody who knew her would believe how badly she had been in love with Kosta. She had hidden it well and she was going to carry on hiding it. And nobody would look any deeper because they all knew that Bella Carew was a flirt who had no deep feelings to speak of. And they were damned well going to keep on knowing it, she resolved grimly.

She led the way back into Annis's elegant sitting room and flung herself onto the sofa. She kicked off her shoes and tucked her feet under her.

'So tell me who's going to be at this bash of yours, if it's not the whole of English society.'

Annis pulled a face. 'It's a small church, fortunately. That's the only constraint Lynda has taken any notice of. There's going to be a couple of hundred, all told. Kosta's family are coming in from all over the world, of course.'

'Nice,' said Bella without interest. 'Have you asked Gil the Client?'

'Yes, as a matter of fact.' Annis looked at her shrewdly. 'Don't you like him?'

Bella shrugged. 'What's to like? He looked like boring businessman, standard issue to me.' She was really, really proud of her indifferent tone.

Annis was totally unsuspicious. She laughed. 'You should hear the way his staff talk about him. They think he's somewhere between Robin Hood and the god Apollo.'

'Really?'

'Well, he's trying to rescue his company and save their jobs at the moment,' Annis explained.

Bella pulled a face. 'Yeah, well. Not exactly civilisation as we know it, is it? Some piffling company!'

'It's not piffling' said Annis indignantly. 'Gil has put together cutting edge technology. Plus, he's committed to giving the major stake to the guys who do the work, not some clever financial predators. I think he's a bit of a hero myself.'

Bella buried her nose in her coffee, not answering. Part of her was exultant at this praise. She had no idea why and that made the other part of her—the older, wiser part—distinctly uneasy.

'So tell me about my bridesmaid's dress,' she said, reverting to party-girl mode.

'It's a caftan like mine, only it's blue.'

Bella stayed suspicious. 'Powder-blue? Like little girls' party dresses.'

'No, no,'' Annis assured her. 'It's a very sophisticated colour.'

Bella pursed her lips. 'We-ell,' she said, in mock negotiation. 'No tulle. No lace, right?'

Annis bit back a smile. 'No tulle. No lace,' she agreed gravely.

'All right, then, I'll wear it. I brought a designer dress from New York. But I can keep that for the dance afterwards. There is going to be a dance afterwards?'

'You know your mother too well,' said Annis ruefully. 'We said no. She took no notice. There's a dance.'

'Great,' said Bella with enthusiasm. Lots of music and old friends to dance with meant that, with a bit of luck, she could keep her conversation with Kosta down to the minimum.

'You and your parties,' said Annis affectionately. 'Lynda said half the county has been on the phone asking how long you're staying over.'

Bella shook her head decisively. 'Plane back on Sunday. I've got a career to think about, these days. Now show me that dress. I warn you, any hint of frou frou and I'm in my Big Apple number.'

But it was a slim silken robe, peacock shot with turquoise, edged at the neck and sleeves with gold braid.

'Very peace and love,' said Bella, turning this way and that to survey her image in Annis's new mirror.

'I thought it had better not be too close fitting as you weren't here to try it on,' her stepsister explained.

'Good thinking, Bat Woman. Let's see yours.'

Annis was going to wear a loose robe, too, though hers was a creamy brocade sewn with pearls.

'Scrumptious,' said Bella without envy. 'Just right with your height. How clever of you. When did this passion for Oriental robes start?'

Annis bit her lip. 'I wanted to talk to you about that.'

Bella was alarmed. 'It's not going to be some summer solstice number, is it? I mean, I'll do whatever you want but I was expecting a bog standard wedding. Flowers, aisle, couple of rings, couple of hymns and we all make a break for the champers. Anything else and I'll need a crash course.'

'No, no,' said Annis amused. 'It's a classic English wedding. But my measurements have been a bit—er—uncertain. In fact, there's something else I ought to tell you—'

Only then the telephone rang. Annis answered and had a brief conversation. As soon as she put it down, it rang again.

It went on for the best part of an hour.

'Sorry,' she said, making a face while she held on for the man at the other end to find some figures. 'Gil is just coming up to a major launch. He's been struggling to keep the lid on it for weeks. He wanted to announce it at the end of April. But it looks like all hell is breaking loose today.'

'Oh?' Bella could not have sounded more bored. She was proud of that.

Annis nodded. 'He's probably going to have to call a press conference. He'll hate that.'

Bella wandered round the room. 'Doesn't like publicity?

'Doesn't like doing anything until he has thoroughly prepared himself. Gil never does anything until he's ready.'

Oh no? thought Bella. The voice whispered in her ear again. *'Let me come up.'* 'Sounds boring.'

'Lovely guy but not your type,' conceded Annis.

She went back to her telephone conversation. Bella picked up a brides' magazine and leafed through it. She barely saw the pictures, though.

Was he not her type? Why? Annis's throw-away remark annoyed her. She did not know why, either, and that annoyed her even more. After all, her heart had been broken when Kosta had turned her away. It did not matter if Gil de la Court was her type or she was his.

When Annis finally finished her business, Bella cast the magazine aside and stood up.

'I ought to be getting home.'

Bella still had her old room in her parents' elegant house.

'Must you? We haven't really talked yet.'

'Not much chance of that from the looks of it,' said Bella without rancour.

'With me up to my eyebrows in Gil de la Court's press announcement, you mean.' Annis looked harassed. 'I'm really sorry. It couldn't have happened at a worse time.'

'Don't worry about it. We'll get together later.'

Annis looked even more harassed. 'Well, there's a problem with that. Kosta's parents are in town and we're doing a rush job of getting to know each other. I don't suppose you want to come to a family meal with them tonight?'

'No,' said Bella in tones of horror.

'No,' said Annis with understanding.

The telephone rang.

'Get that,' said Bella, picking up her bag and the elegantly packed bridesmaid's dress. 'I'll get the alterations done and we can talk later.'

Annis was on the phone again by the time she let herself out. It felt very strange.

But nothing like as strange as it was to get home and find, instead of her usual full royalty welcome, her mother barely had time to give her a distracted kiss of welcome. Lynda Carew had tried very hard to persuade her stepdaughter to have the wedding of the century. She'd planned an abbey ceremony, a reception in a medieval castle, a dance for a thousand people afterwards, and fireworks at midnight. When this met with united opposition from Annis, Kosta and the bride's father, Lynda decided to throw her considerable organisational talents into contriving the most stylish small wedding possible. With a mere two hundred guests to think about, she had compiled a dossier on all the major guests and a three-day timetable, broken down into half-hour units.

Bella caused the first breach in the timetable by retiring to soak in the bath as soon as she had taken the bridesmaid's dress for its alterations. She was only just emerging when her mother and stepfather left for their dinner with Kosta's family.

Bella came out onto the landing wrapped in her bath towel to kiss them goodbye.

'Are you sure you'll be all right?' said Lynda anxiously.

'Glad of an early night,' Bella assured her.

'Don't fuss,' said Tony Carew gruffly. 'She can pig out on pizza and children's videos.'

Bella did not deny it. Almost as soon as her mother had remarried, Bella had found that she and her new stepfather shared a passion for children's movies that neither of the other two could understand. She grinned. '*Railway Children* here I come.'

When they had gone, her smiled died. This wedding, she thought, was going to be more difficult than she had imagined. And she had expected it to be bad enough.

She wrapped herself in her old dressing gown from school and trailed up to the old nursery she had shared with Annis. She wandered round, drawing stuff off the shelves at random.

They were all there—her favourite books, the battered rabbit, the shared dolls that Annis had dressed for her, the jigsaw puzzle of Windsor Castle, the box of water-colours with no turquoise left because that had always been her favourite colour...

Bella swallowed.

Downstairs the doorbell rang.

At first she was tempted to ignore it. But then she thought it must be her parents, returning to collect a forgotten door key or something. The bell rang again, imperatively. Yes, that was definitely Tony, impatient at being kept waiting.

She ran down the stairs, bare feet slipping in her haste.

'Left the family dossiers behind?' she teased, flinging open the door and hanging onto it.

For the second time that day she came face

to face with Gil de la Court.

'Oh!'

Gil had not been able to believe it when he'd first realised who was in the photograph at Annis's flat. For a while he had even accused himself of hallucinating, so obsessed that he couldn't put the girl out of his mind, even when he was in the middle of life-and-death negotiations.

But he soon realised that it was no mirage. In fact, he realised more than that. He must have been looking at the photograph during his visits to this room for months, without really taking it in. That had to be the reason why he had taken one look at the girl in the nightclub and had felt that pull of recognition. Well, part of the reason. And of course the pull he had felt was more than recognition. A lot more.

While Annis was putting together some staff simulations for year three of Watifdotcom, he picked up the silver-framed picture.

It had been taken at a picnic. There were the parents, whom he had met. There was Annis, long-legged in jeans. And there was his fate. Younger, rounder, with soft hair all over the place and a wide schoolgirl grin but still, unmistakeably, the fire-ball blonde of his dreams.

'Your sister?' he said to Annis, quite as if he didn't care.

'Yes, that's Bella.'

Bella. He savoured the name. His Bella. And now he knew how to find her.

That was when he said goodbye to the plans he had been considering for tracking her down. Some of them were quite dramatic. Just as well, he thought with private self-mockery. He was not sure how Bella would respond to a mariachi band under her New York window.

Now he did not have to serenade her from the street. She would have to come back for the wedding. So then he could go and knock at her door—a nice, familiar London door—and point out that they were made for each other. Well, he would give her a bit of time to get used to him and then he would point it out. Or better still he would get himself invited to the wedding. Very infectious, weddings.

At last he could concentrate on his company rescue plan with a clear mind.

It never occurred to him to wonder how Bella would react when she saw him.

But as soon as she arrived, he saw that it would be pointless to try to talk to her in front of Annis. Worse than pointless, he realised, seeing her look of shock and the dawning temper.

Oh, yes, his Tina the Tango Dancer was not at all pleased about this turn of events.

So he kept his face neutral and his conversation brief. He could feel Bella's frustration as the door of the flat closed behind him.

He bit back a smile. Tonight, he promised himself. Tonight.

When he stood on the Carew doorstep, he paused for a second before ringing the bell. What would she be handing out tonight? Not welcome, he was fairly sure. Well, not to begin with. Later, when she had forgiven him for finding her unforgettable—and then finding her—maybe. Gil braced himself for a fiery blonde rage with some anticipation.

And then she opened the door and he was silenced.

Elderly dressing gown? Bare feet? This was not his wild salsa babe. She was not even the wary city girl he had duelled with in the February night. She wore no make-up, no defences and she was laughing at whomever she expected to see at the doorstep. It was not him.

Gil watched the laughter die out of her face. It was like walking into a wall. Her withdrawal hit him like a Siberian winter.

'And hello to you too,' he said, recovering.

Bella pulled herself together and pushed a hand through her loose hair. She felt wrong-footed and vulnerable and it made her mad.

'What are you doing here?' she said in her most disagreeable tone.

He was unimpressed. 'You must have realised I'd come as soon as I could get away.'

'Of course I didn't.'

'Then, you are a lot more naïve than your sister says you are,' he said with perfect calm. 'Are you going to let me in or shall we shout at each other on the doorstep?'

'I am not shouting,' yelled Bella.

He smiled.

She pulled the old dressing tighter round her and took a firm grip on the door.

'I don't know what you're doing here—'

'Yes, you do.'

Bella ignored the interruption. 'But I'm getting over a transatlantic flight and a rough day. I'm going to have an early night.'

His dark smile was pure provocation. 'Sounds good.'

Bella was used to dealing with male provocation. Before her departure for New York she had been known as one of the biggest flirts in London. It was not so easy to repel flirtation in a felt dressing gown, with hair damp from the bath and no make-up or shoes. But she made a gallant attempt.

'In your dreams.'

'You are so right. How are yours?'

'My what?'

He leaned against the door jamb as if he was going to stay there all night. 'Dreams.'

'My dreams are fine, thank you.'

'You must tell me all about them,' he said politely. 'Now, are you going to let me in?'

'Why should I?'

'Because this time you know who I am. You can afford to risk it.'

Bella narrowed her eyes at him. 'You're saying that I would have let you in last time if I had known who you were?'

'Sure.'

'And why would I have done that?'

'Because this happens once in a lifetime.'

'You must have led a very sheltered life.

Gil ignored that. He leaned in towards her. His voice sank. It was horribly intimate.

'Tina the Tango Dancer knew. Where has she gone?'

Their eyes met. Something in his dark glance made the smart remark on the tip of her tongue melt away as if she had never thought of it. Bella shivered—and was silenced.

He straightened.

'You're cold,' he said in quite a different voice.

'I—' About to deny it, she paused. It was a better reason for shivering than the only other one that presented itself. She stood back. 'You'd better come in.'

She took him into her mother's elegant drawing room, with its pale sofas and collectors' art in discreetly lit alcoves. He did not spare them a glance.

That unnerved Bella. Usually people were impressed by her home. Well, at least they noticed it. Gil de la Court did not take his eyes off her long enough to register a single priceless piece.

Bella cleared her throat. 'Well?'

'Why didn't you call me?'

'Why should I?'

'We had unfinished business.'

She met his eyes defiantly. 'I don't remember that.'

'You got my flowers. You had my number. All my numbers, God help me. Why didn't you get in touch? I told you to.'

'Could be you've just answered your own question.'

He stared at her for an incredulous moment. 'What?'

'I don't take orders,' announced Bella.

She did not understand herself. Normally she was co-operative to a fault. It was Annis who dug her heels in and refused to be ordered around. Bella was the sunny peacemaker. But this man did not make her feel like a peacemaker.

'That's just petty—'

'*Particularly* orders from someone I don't know.'

He shook his head, bewildered. 'We'd talked. You knew as much about me as I knew about you.'

'I didn't know your name. When you were giving me your orders you left that bit out.'

He brushed that aside. 'You knew more of my name than I knew of yours.'

'Quite,' said Bella triumphantly. 'I'm a modern woman. I protect myself from stalkers.'

There was a short, fraught silence.

He said levelly, 'You knew I wasn't a stalker. Or you wouldn't have agreed to have coffee with me that night.'

'That was before you tried to talk yourself back into my flat,' Bella flung at him.

Rash. Very rash. She realised it as soon as she saw him smile.

'So you *do* remember.'

She did. Oh, indeed she did. Bella went hot, cold, then hot again.

This man is not going to make me blush, she vowed. *He is* not.

'I think it's time you went.'

He did not move. 'Coward,' he said softly.

She refused to meet his eyes. 'Not at all. My family—'

'Are all dining with the overseas visitors. You don't expect them back for several hours.'

She choked, 'How on earth do you know that?'

'Annis told me,' he said coolly.

Bella could not think of anything to say.

'You've been spying on me,' she managed, just a little too late. Also the tone of outrage sounded false, even to her own ears.

'Just acquiring basic information,' he corrected. 'Frankly, I don't have the time for a decent surveillance job at the moment.'

Bella gasped. '*Don't have the time!* Are you apologising for *not* spying on me?'

'Well, you clearly want me to apologise for something. It might as well be true.'

'I don't,' she said between her teeth, 'want you to apologise for one damned thing.'

Which, of course, made him a present of exactly the opportunity he was looking for.

'Great,' he said briskly. 'That's got that out of the way. Now, let's talk about where we go from here.'

Bella drew herself to her full height. It would have been easier if she had not been barefoot but she was beyond caring.

'*I*,' she said with emphasis, 'am going to bed. You—'

He interrupted again. She should have known he would.

'Not yet. Great idea but it's too soon.'

She stared at him, too stunned even to be angry for a moment.

He gave her an odiously kind smile. 'We will. I promise. Just not tonight.'

There was a moment when Bella very nearly threw a Meissen porcelain shepherdess at him. Only the fact that he took her by the arm and steered her away from the potential missile prevented her.

'You will agree with me when you think about it,' he added helpfully.

Bella spluttered. 'I won't—'

'Flattering,' he said, amused. 'But we don't want to rush things.'

'That isn't what I meant and you know it,' Bella shouted.

'Now, show me where the kitchen is. You are definitely cold. We must get you a hot drink.'

She wrenched her arm out of his hold.

'I am not cold and I don't want a hot drink. How old do you think I am?'

He took that seriously. It gave him the opportunity to let his eyes wander all the way down her. Then all the way up again. Bella found she was pulling the dressing gown together hard and scraping one foot up the back of her leg in her unease.

He said coolly, 'Oh, somewhere between four-and-a-half and several centuries.'

Bella was so confused, she forgot how angry she was. She stared at him blankly.

'What? Why?'

'Your eyes,' he said with perfect sang-froid. 'Old as Cleopatra and twice as dangerous.'

Bella's mouth fell open. Men didn't say things like that. *Nobody* said things like that.

Gil was quite unembarrassed. 'But nobody stands on one leg after they leave kindergarten,' he added kindly.

Bella hurriedly returned her foot to the floor.

His mouth stayed steady but his eyes were laughing. 'That explain the age range to your satisfaction?'

'Yes,' she said dazedly. 'I suppose so. I mean—you're not crazy, are you?'

It was his turn to look blank.

'Excuse me?'

Bella realised that she had the chance to get some of the initiative back. She grabbed it with both hands.

'Dad says some of Annis's clients are real lulus,' she said artlessly. 'Brilliant but barking. Are you very clever, Mr de la Court?'

Their eyes met. Bella widened hers into a look of sweet enquiry. There was a sizzling pause.

Then he gave a reluctant laugh. 'Call me Gil. It's easier to insult someone when you're on first-name terms.'

Bella managed to look shocked. 'But I don't want to insult you.'

'Yes, you do. But you'll get over it.'

Bella choked on a laugh. She fought it down. 'Really?'

'Everyone does. Believe me.'

It was like being out in the sun when he smiled at her like that. She could have thrown her arms wide and basked in it. Even though he was as unpredictable as quicksilver and tricky with it. There was a caressing note in the teasing voice. It teased but at the same time it beckoned, luring her to go down some path she had never sensed before. It might even lead to paradise.

Bella found herself leaning towards him slowly, slowly… Their eyes locked…

She caught herself just in time.

'Wow.' She breathed.

Was he startled too? Just for a moment she thought Gil de la Court looked a lot less amused. Bella drew a shaken breath.

'What do you want?' she whispered.

'You.'

His eyes had an odd, stunned look. Bella did not think he was lying. She did not think he was capable of lying at this moment.

She swallowed hard. 'This is not a great idea.'

But she could not tear her eyes away.

And then he really shocked her.

He put his hand out and brushed the tangled hair away from her face. It was an odd gesture, clumsy and uncontrolled. She did not think it was what he had meant to do. It had just happened, somehow.

It was not the clumsiness that was shocking. It was the tenderness. Bella went as still as if she had been turned to stone.

'Bella,' he said, as if he was tasting her name.

'Gil, you don't know me,' she said loudly.

She had to break the mood. She *had* to.

'What?'

He was looking at her mouth as if he was going to draw it.

'You danced with me once. You kissed me once. You sent me some flowers. You don't know me.' She was almost frantic.

His eyes flickered. He did not step back but he did not kiss her. Bella found she was desperate for him not to kiss her. She could not understand it, she had kissed hundreds of men. It was as easy as breathing. But Gil was different. He made her melt just to look at him but she was not ready for another of those hair-raising kisses. Well, not yet.

Not ready? Not *yet*? This was serious.

'You don't know a thing about me,' said Bella, gabbling. She did not add that, just at the moment, she did not know much about herself either. She shook her head helplessly.

'Then, tell me.'

'I—'

'You're scared, aren't you?' He sounded fascinated.

That brought her to her senses. She was the most popular babe on the block. She knew all there was to know about sex. She could handle men. She could handle this.

'Of course I'm not scared.'

'Then, tell me all this stuff I don't know about you.'

Bella pulled herself together. 'Darling, I'd love to. But I'm only in London until Sunday night. My sister's getting married, you know.'

He ignored the irony. 'Fine. Let me drive you down to the wedding.'

Her composure fell apart. 'I can't. I mean, I'm going down to the country early. Tomorrow. My mother needs me—'

He said softly, 'Scared.'

Bella stiffened. 'I am not,' she said, 'scared of you or anyone.'

'Not of me. Yourself.'

'Scared I won't keep my hands off you, you mean?' she said scornfully. 'What a dreamer!'

His eyes glinted. 'Then, prove me wrong.'

She knew she was being manipulated. Of course she did. But Bella had never run away from a challenge in her life. She was not starting now.

Her chin tilted. 'OK. Be here tomorrow at three. If you're not, I'll go on my own.'

She had a feeling from what Annis had said about him being so busy, he had no time for anything. So surely he would not be able to walk away from all that high-powered negotiation for a whole Friday afternoon?

Gil did not hesitate for a second.

'I'll be here.'

CHAPTER FIVE

THE car backed neatly into the space in front of the house at three o'clock on the dot.

'Here he is,' said her mother, evidently relieved. She had been piling cases and bags and dress boxes in the entrance hall since lunchtime.

'He made it, then,' said Bella in an odd voice.

Her mother looked at her in surprise. 'Did you think he would stand you up?'

'He shouldn't be here at all. I spoke to Annis this morning. She said he had to stick around for press queries. He's launching his company on the stock market today.'

'That's nice.'

'But it means he isn't free to drive me anywhere,' pointed out Bella. 'Or he shouldn't be. He's playing truant.'

'Perhaps he wants to,' said Lynda, amused.

Bella did not answer that directly. She watched the tall man get out of the limousine. 'I've never known anyone like him,' she said almost to herself.

Lynda restacked a couple of shoe boxes.

'Well, actually, your father and I were really glad that he offered to take you down to the country.'

'I can imagine,' Bella agreed drily.

Her mother had never once mentioned Bella's feelings for her imminent brother-in-law, had never even admitted the possibility, but her anxiety was palpable. *Perhaps she knows*, thought Bella, shocked. *Perhaps maternal instinct has struck again.* She writhed inwardly at the thought.

But Lynda was thinking of something else entirely. 'We haven't said anything, of course, and I'm sure Annis doesn't know, but we thought at one time he might not go to the wedding at all.'

That brought Bella out of her self-absorption. She turned startled eyes on her mother.

'What?'

'He hasn't said anything. And I could be wrong, of course.'

'What are you talking about?'

Gil was coming up the garden path.

Lynda said hurriedly, 'We just thought he was a bit cut up about Annis getting married. He didn't come to the engagement party.'

Bella nearly said, I know he didn't. If he had I would have known him when he came to New York.

She didn't. She said in a stupefied voice, 'Gil de la Court is in love with *Annis*?'

The doorbell rang.

'Oh, I wouldn't go that far,' said Lynda, flustered. 'They just say that he always keeps women at arm's length. Only he didn't do it to Annis. Some people said—well, it doesn't matter now. Will you get the door, darling? I'll just get the veil from upstairs.'

She darted out into the hallway.

'Who, Mother?' said Bella following her. 'Who said?'

But Lynda was halfway up the stairs and the doorbell rang again. Bella gave up and opened the door.

She looked at him blankly.

Gil smiled. He looked very handsome in his restrained city suit. His dark hair was just a little too long, a little too untidy. And his eyes were not restrained at all.

But all he said was, 'Ready?'

He did not offer to kiss her, Bella noticed.

She said composedly, 'Yes, I'm all packed. My mother would like us to take quite a load with us. If you don't have room, of course, we can leave it.'

'There's room.'

He gestured to the car. Bella looked. Saw that the dark limousine was enormous. Probably the last word in luxurious comfort, she thought.

'So I see. You like to travel in style.'

He gave a soft laugh. 'Why does that sound like an insult?' he said in wonder. 'No, I don't normally drive a souped-up pantechnicon. I thought you'd probably bring a mountain of bags and we wouldn't get them in my own car. This one's rented.'

Bella bit her lip.

'Forward thinking.' There was a slight edge to her voice.

'Focus,' he corrected.

'I'm impressed.' She held the door open. 'Do you want to come in or shall we go at once?'

'The sooner the better.'

Did that mean he did not want to spend time talking to Lynda? Had he detected that she had found out his secret?

But then Lynda came downstairs balancing the huge box that held the wedding veil and he greeted her with no sign of embarrassment.

She surrendered the box to him. 'Gil, it's so good of you to drive Bella.' She gave him a warm hug. 'I wish we could offer to put you up. But the house is full.'

'Don't worry about it. I'm with the bachelor party in Priory Court.'

Lynda laughed and let him go. 'Don't let them play any horrible tricks on Kosta tonight.'

'I'll do my best.'

He took the box out to the car and unlocked the boot. Bella followed with more boxes and her overnight case. She stood on the pavement, and watched him load. He put everything into the car with geometric precision. *Focus*, she thought. His fingers were long and deft. She gave a little shiver and stepped back.

'I'll just say goodbye to Mother and we can get going.'

On the doorstep Lynda hugged her, her eyes suspiciously bright. 'Don't get lost, darling. I'll see you at dinner. Our last dinner with just the family.'

Bella gulped but said bravely, 'And about time too. How long did you want your daughters on your hands?'

She kissed Lynda's cheek and ran.

Gil held the door for her before swinging into the driver's seat.

'"Don't get lost"?' he echoed.

Bella blinked rapidly. Why on earth had Lynda suddenly gone soggy like that? Damn it, Annis was not even walking down the aisle and here Bella was, choking up.

'Family joke,' she said curtly, turning her head away.

Gil did not ask directions. He slid the big car through the narrow one-way system as if he was a professional chauffeur and knew every inch of the winding streets.

'Pretend I'm one of the family, then,' he said drily.

Bella hunted in her handbag and brought out a tissue. She blew her nose rather loudly.

'Oh, I was always known for missing my way. Dad bought me a car for my twenty-first but he couldn't buy me a sense of direction. I used to set out all right. And then there would be something on the radio—or I'd be listening to a new CD—or there would be a wonderful sunset—and I'd end up somewhere I didn't mean to go.'

'Sounds interesting.'

She gave a little choke of laughter. 'Yes, for me. Tough on the others, though. They'd all be sitting round waiting for me to arrive so they could start dinner. Mother would have me at the bottom of a motorway pile-up until I called in and gave them my grid reference.'

'Sounds like you were a handful.'

She sighed. 'I suppose I was.'

'Is that was why your mother is so glad I'm doing the driving today?'

She almost jumped. 'You picked that up?'

'It didn't take a lot of picking it up.'

'I suppose not,' Bella admitted, reluctantly.

'And that's why?'

'Probably,' she hedged.

She did not want to talk about Lynda's sympathy or his possible feelings for Annis. She was surprised by how fiercely she did not want to talk about them.

'Not like Annis, then.'

It was as if he was reading her mind. She slewed round in her seat to look at him. *'What?'*

She could see that he was biting back a smile. 'If you were a rebel. Annis always tells me that she was a terminally good girl.'

He sounded amused, affectionate.

But—in love?

Bella could not decide. She said, 'Well, not exactly a rebel. Just not as together as Annis.'

Gil laughed. 'Nobody is as together as Annis.'

That affection again! But was it the sort of thing you said about the woman you were in love with? More important, was it the sort of thing Gil said about the woman *he* was in love with?

Bella said carefully, 'How did you meet?'

'I was an academic with a good idea and no business know-how. Annis came up with the goods.' He smiled reminiscently. 'Actually she came up with a lot more advice than I thought

I wanted at the time. Shook me to my foundations. It's really thanks to her that Watifdotcom is going public today.'

Bella digested this. 'So you've known each other for ages?'

'Not at all. It's been short but intense.'

Intense?

'Oh.'

They hit a roundabout and he fell silent as he negotiated the fast, heavy traffic. He did not speak again until they were on the motorway.

'So how long have you been in New York and what do you do there?' He slid her a sideways looks, inviting her to share his amusement. 'We've got a lot of blank spaces to fill in for people who have come so far.'

Oh, no, we haven't, thought Bella. *We haven't come any distance at all. I didn't know that you ever had any interest in my sister Annis. As for me—what you don't know about me would fill a book. Just as well if that's the way it stays, too.*

But, unlike Annis, she was the sociable one. She knew how to chatter obligingly without giving away one single thing of importance. She did just that for the rest of the journey.

By the time they got to the Gothic mansion that was the Carew country house, her mouth was dry and she was running out of small talk.

Gil had been silent for the last twenty miles, except to ask directions. She had the impression that he was as relieved as she was when they drove up the sweep of the gravelled drive.

He parked under an overhanging rhododendron and turned off the engine. For a moment he seemed lost in thought. Then he turned to her.

'What's wrong?' he said quietly.

'Wrong? Nothing.' Even to Bella the bright tone sounded forced. 'I'm really grateful for the lift.'

'Will I see you tonight?'

She spread her hands. 'You heard Lynda. Last meal as a family. I can't walk out on that.'

He looked impatient. 'Of course not. I mean afterwards.'

'After dinner?'

'No need to sound so shocked. I assume you won't go on eating to midnight.'

'No but—' She was floundering.

He took both her hands. 'Which is your room?'

Oh no, she thought. *Here we go again: 'Let me come up.'*

'Thinking of climbing up to my chamber?' she said with heavy irony. It almost disguised her breathlessness at the very thought.

'If that's what it takes.'

'Takes?'

'To make you talk to me.'

Bella removed her hands. 'I've been talking to you all the way down here.'

'No, you haven't. You've been talking at me.'

She was silenced.

'See what I mean?' he said drily. 'One flash of honesty and all the bright chatter dries up, doesn't it?'

Bella's chin went up. 'I'm sorry if I bored you.'

Quite suddenly Gil turned away and slammed his fist into the steering wheel, making her jump. 'You didn't bore me,' he said between clenched teeth.

She watched his fist warily. 'Then, why are you so angry?' She sounded breathless, even to her own ears.

He did not answer for a minute. Then he said heavily, 'You don't give an inch, do you?'

She did not pretend to misunderstand. 'Isn't that my privilege?'

'But *why*?'

She shrugged, looking away.

'Anyone would think I meant to hurt you,' he said furiously.

Bella did not make a movement. She knew she did not. But he straightened, suddenly alert.

'That's it, isn't it? That's why you won't let me get close to you.'

Bella tried hard to laugh. 'Rubbish.'

He ignored that. 'You think I'll hurt you,' he said on a long note of discovery.

'That's crazy,' said Bella sharply.

'Is it?'

'Of course it is.'

He shook his head, ignoring that too. 'What on earth did I do?' he said almost to himself.

'Nothing.' Her voice rose. 'It's all in your imagination.'

'Or maybe—' He stopped.

'What?'

'Maybe it's got nothing to do with me. Maybe it's you. Has someone done a number on you, Bella?'

'No.' It was almost a scream. She took hold of herself. 'No.'

Gil looked at her searchingly. 'Sure?'

'Of course I'm sure.'

'No man has let you down? Deceived you?'

Oh, but he was persistent. Was this how he ran that fantastic business of his? By digging and dissecting, digging and dissecting…

She stayed calm but it was an effort. Her jaw ached with it.

'No.'

'Walked out on you?'

She could not take any more of this. Deliberately she tossed back her hair, knowing that its scent would waft around him in the close confines of the car. She saw his eyes flicker and bit back her relief.

'Do I look the sort of girl that a man would walk out on?' she said lightly. 'I don't mean to be vain—but get real.'

It gave him pause. She seized her chance. Briskly she unclasped her seat belt before he could start any more of that too shrewd analysis.

'I must get going. There'll be plenty of last-minute panics if I know my mother.'

She did not risk another glance at him. Instead she pushed the passenger door open and got out. Gil followed without comment.

As he did so, the front door opened. Gil stopped, startled.

'How did that happen? Sensors?'

'The housekeeper being discreet,' said Bella, torn between fury and reluctant amusement.

'What?'

'She was here long before my mother and I arrived on the scene. Tony trained her. He doesn't like fuss. So she doesn't do any of that apple-cheeked housekeeper welcome stuff. She just hovers until we start unloading.'

She pushed the door back on its hinges and gathered the self-effacing housekeeper into a comprehensive hug.

'Hi, Ruth. Oh, it's so good to be back.'

The housekeeper returned the hug. 'Bella, my lamb. Let me look at you.' She held her away. 'So glamorous.'

'That's New York polish for you,' said Bella grinning. 'I suppose I'm a jet-setter now.'

She had her cheek patted for her pains. 'Ah, but you've still got eyes like a bush-baby. Just like you always did. I'm so *glad* that you could make it to the wedding after all.'

Gil, coming up with suitcases, raised an eyebrow.

Bella said hastily, 'Ruth, do you know Gil de la Court?'

Ruth looked alarmed. 'I've heard Annis speak of you of course. But I didn't realise you'd be here today—'

'Don't worry,' he said reassuringly. 'I'm delivering, not staying. Just tell me where you want the luggage and I'll be on my way.'

But when he had unloaded the car, he did not go quite at once. Bella stood in the echoing marble entrance hall willing him to but he did not. He inspected the tapestries, the branched candlesticks, even the portraits, as if he was a casual tourist and she had all the time in the world to show him round.

'Look,' she said, 'I hate to seem inhospitable but there's a lot to do.'

He turned away from a marvellously cuffed cavalier and surveyed her with the same narrow-eyed assessment.

'Don't turn the bush-baby look on me,' he told her, suddenly crisp. 'I don't melt. And if I did, you're no cuddly toy.'

Bella gaped.

He strode over to her. His shoes clipped the marble, staccato in the silence.

He looked down at her for a moment as if he were measuring an opponent.

He said softly, 'Never forget. I've seen the way you dance. Heaven help me, I've *felt* the way you dance. Whatever these people here may think about you, I know you.'

Bella felt her face flame. But she managed to say steadily, 'That sounds like a threat.'

'Call it a reminder.'

'A reminder of what?' she said unwarily.

His eyes flicked to her mouth and he laughed.

She thought, *He's going to kiss me again.*

Suddenly she wanted him to. She wanted him to grab her, as he had on that frozen street in New York. She wanted him to turn her into nothing but sensation, make her body tune out her brain. For a while, at least. She wanted it with an intensity that shocked her.

And he turned away.

He turned away.

'See you,' he said casually.

And was gone.

Bella sat down hard on the bottom stair. She felt as if all the breath had been knocked out of her.

She had wanted him to kiss her. He knew she had wanted him to kiss her. And he had walked away.

All that talk about wanting to get close to her and he had walked away!

It had been quite deliberate. Bella knew that. Until last year she had run with a crowd where such tactics were commonplace. She had never expected to find herself on the receiving end of a move like that, though.

Well, she wasn't going to. She didn't want it and she didn't have to put up with it. Gil de la Court wasn't going to play games with her head. In fact, Gil de la Court was going to be very lucky if she ever spoke to him again.

She did not tell anyone, though. She told herself that she did not want to get into an argument about making a guest feel welcome. But secretly she knew it was more than that.

Her mother had already hinted that he was in love with Annis. Bella did not want to find herself put in charge of distracting the spurned lover during the wedding festivities. But if Lynda had that in mind, then she would want an explanation before she let Bella off the hook.

Bella found that she really, *really* didn't want to talk to anyone about her private dealings with Gil de la Court. She did not want to have to admit that she had met him before. That she had not been able to put him out of her mind. That, once, he had touched her and had turned her bones to water. That every time she saw him, she quivered with awareness that he could, just possibly, do it again.

It was sex, she told herself fiercely. That was all it was, that time in New York. Hormones and opportunity and a great big dollop of loneliness.

And since? prompted the uncomfortably honest part of her mind. What was it in London when he touched you? And in the hall here, when he didn't?

'*Games!*' said Bella aloud.

It made her so mad she could have thrown things. But it also made her jumpy. This wedding had promised to be difficult enough, without some sexy circling by Gil de la Court. Who just might be breaking his heart over her sister. She winced at the thought.

It didn't feel as if he was breaking his heart, Bella thought rebelliously. *Not the way he looked at Annis, not the way he looks at me. To say nothing of the way he kisses me.*

But, then again, she knew Gil de la Court played games. Hell, she had first-hand experience, didn't she? Maybe he was deliberately trying to distract himself with someone, anyone, who wasn't Annis. Bella was just the first woman who came to hand.

No, it was more than that. Even in her wretched muddle, she knew that. She intrigued him. She knew she did. There was no game of pretend about that.

But did she want to intrigue him?

A part of her said no. That was the honest, straightforward part that wanted Annis to be happy. That was the part that wanted to get through the wedding with dignity intact and then head for the hills before anyone could ask, 'And what is happening in your love life these days, Bella? Still playing the field, ha ha?'

But a darker, more reckless part said *yes.*

She did not understand it. She did not want it. She did her best to suppress it.

In the process she went very quiet. Among all the wedding preparations, however, no one noticed.

They were all much more worried about Annis, who was not only quiet but much too pale. She arrived later than anyone expected and was uncharacteristically terse when Lynda showed concern.

'Don't *fuss*. I can't bear fuss.'

'But we thought you would be here for tea. We were worried.'

'I would have been here for tea if Gilbert de la Court had been where he ought to have been,' said Annis, with concentrated fury. 'Instead of which, you roped him in to play chauffeur and I've had a running skirmish with the financial press all afternoon.'

Then she burst into tears and fled to her room.

'Overtired,' said Lynda into the uncomfortable silence.

There were ten for dinner that night and, whatever they might politely pretend, every one of the guests must have overheard the spat in the entrance hall. They were all family, or as good as, but even so there was some uncomfortable shuffling of feet.

Lynda sent her daughter a beseeching look. 'Bella, would you—?'

Bella went.

Annis had the big corner room on the second floor. Bella tapped on the door.

'Who is it?' Her voice was muffled but at least she did not sound as if she was crying any longer.

'Me. Can I come in, Annie?'

There was the sound of the key turning in the lock. Annis sniffed but she stood aside to let Bella pass.

'Sorry,' she said. 'Lost it a bit, back there.'

'Are you all right?' said Bella, concerned.

To her dismay, her sister's eyes filled with tears again. She put her arms round her.

'Hey there, Brain Box.'

'I don't know what's wrong with me,' wailed Annis.

'Hush. You've just got wedding nerves.'

Annis gulped and muttered something incomprehensible.

'Everyone does. Part of the ritual,' Bella assured her, patting one heaving shoulder. She kept talking, giving Annis time to pull herself together. 'Every time one of our staffers does an "I was the bride's right-hand man" piece, they come back with copy that's full of mayhem. Downright war, sometimes.'

Annis straightened and turned away, searching her dressing table for the box of paper tissues.

'I didn't know that. Everything I've read about weddings has been full of amazing flowers and perfect arrangements. This is going to be a shambles.'

'No, it's not.'

Annis blew her nose pugnaciously. 'Yes, it is. My dress looks ridiculous and my shoes are too wide. I'll probably lose one going up the aisle.'

'Then, I'll field it. That's what bridesmaids are for.'

Annis glared at her. 'By then I will have fallen over. Your mother has organised the aisle like an assault course. Great bunches of flowers on tripods. I'm bound to knock one of them over. I'll probably end up skidding to the altar on my bottom.'

'Then Kosta will pick you up,' said Bella, amused.

'Oh, yes, *he'll* pick me up. *He'll* be looking wonderful,' said Annis, lashing out viciously. 'Every single person in the church will be saying, What on earth does he see in that great clumsy lump of a girl? Oh, *damn*.' Her voice broke.

She stuck her tongue out at her reflection in the dressing-table mirror. Her eyes were much too bright and there were two hectic spots of colour in her pale cheeks.

'He's so damned fanciable. I hate him.'

Bella realised that this was serious. She took Annis by the shoulders and guided her carefully away from the dressing-table mirror to the window seat.

'Now look,' she said, urging Annis onto the cushions, 'this has got to stop.'

Annis blinked sticky lashes at her. 'What?'

'Wedding nerves are fine. Statistically thirty-five per cent of brides have got their cases packed at this stage.'

'What?'

'Latest research findings,' Bella assured her, crossing her fingers behind her back. 'Nerves—not a problem. But slagging off Kosta because he is drop-dead gorgeous is just stupid. And unkind.'

There was a silence.

'Oh,' said Annis at last in a small voice.

'He's in love with you. He doesn't deserve to be blamed for all the things you don't like about yourself.'

Annis's tears subsided in simple indignation.

'When did you get to know everything?' she said belligerently. 'You're supposed to be my baby sister.'

'I've been doing some growing up in New York.'

'Oh, yeah? What's his name?'

'What?'

'Sounds like you've met someone.'

'Don't be silly,' Bella said harshly. Much more harshly than she needed to.

Annis pursed her lips. Suddenly she looked a lot more cheerful.

On the point of denying it heatedly, Bella stopped. She had a blinding revelation. Annis suspected!

Not everything, of course. Not the full disaster of what Bella had felt for Kosta. Not how deep. Not how dangerous. And she sure as hell didn't know what Bella had done about it. But she suspected enough to want Bella to walk down the aisle behind her with all the old shadows blown away. And what better to blow them away than a new man?

This was probably the best wedding present Bella could give her.

Bella's smile twisted. Then she sighed and bowed to the inevitable. 'Yes, I've met someone,' she said.

The irony was that it was even true in an oblique sort of way. Gil de la Court had certainly got under her skin. She was not at all sure what she felt about him but she could not deny the attraction.

The admission did what Annis wanted, anyway. She jumped to her feet and hugged Bella.

'You should have brought him.'

Acutely uncomfortable, Bella muttered, 'No need.'

She did not know why she said that, exactly. Maybe she meant that she did not need the support of an escort to her sister's wedding. Or maybe she meant that, as she was only going to be in England for a few days, there was no point in bringing her mythical lover with her on the long journey. Or maybe— She did not know.

But Annis was looking at her oddly. Bella had the feeling that she had somehow betrayed herself. She just did not know how. Or what. It was crazy.

It was reinforced when Annis squeezed her arm and said soberly, 'It's OK. I can keep my mouth shut. You tell people when you're ready.'

'Thank you,' said Bella. 'I think.'

Annis was herself again. 'So show me the dress. I want to see how good my design skills are.'

Conversation fell back into the important things.

Later Bella went downstairs to reassure her mother. The dinner guests had progressed to coffee and liqueurs in the drawing room and there was a general buzz of relaxed conversation. Clearly Annis's outburst had been swamped by Sole Veronique and Marquise aux Trois Chocolats. To say nothing of Tony's twenty-year-old brandy. No one even looked up when Bella came in.

She went over to her mother's seat by the fire.

'Annis is having an early night,' she murmured in her ear. 'I made her an omelette and she's gone to bed with a mug of cocoa.'

'Cocoa?' Lynda was alarmed. 'She hasn't had that since she was six. She is all right, isn't she?'

'You should see what she's reading,' said Bella, grinning. '*Children of the New Forest.* Complete regression. She's happy as a bug in a rug.'

Lynda still looked worried.

'Honest, Ma. It's just what she needs.'

'Well, if you say so,' said Lynda, surrendering.

'I do. She got herself wound up, that's all. She just needs a bit of cosseting and some space.'

'Space? She's not regretting it?'

'Not for a moment—'

'I mean, if she has any doubts, any at all, she mustn't go through with it. She mustn't feel trapped by the wedding. It's much easier to stop a wedding than get out of a bad marriage,' said Lynda with feeling.

'I know,' said Bella gently. She could—just—remember her own father. She remembered first hand what a bad marriage was like.

'But honestly, I don't think you need to worry, Ma. She's crazy about Kosta.'

Lynda nodded.

Bella knew her mother very well. 'Look, Annis is a grown woman and a brain box. She's not like me. She doesn't do stupid stuff on the spur of the moment.' She added lightly, 'Now, if it were me, you'd be right to be worried.'

Lynda laughed obligingly. But there was still a faint frown between her brows. 'At least you'd know what you were getting into. Annis isn't street smart.'

Bella said sharply, 'Annis is in love.' She sighed. 'Look, Ma. If ever a couple was made for each other it's those two. As you say, I've been around. Enough to know love when I see it. They're ready to commit. Take it from someone who isn't.'

There was a small sound behind her. She looked over her shoulder and went completely blank.

It was Gil de la Court.

CHAPTER SIX

AFTER Bella had got over the simple shock, she found she was indignant. She had told him she did not want to see him tonight.

But Lynda was smiling at him, jumping to her feet and making it perfectly plain that he was the most welcome guest in the world.

'Cuff-links,' she said. 'I put them out as soon as Kosta called.' She waved a hand at her vacated seat. 'Keep Bella amused while I get them.'

'That's going to be an uphill struggle,' murmured Gil.

But he took Lynda's seat and smiled blandly up at Bella, still perched on the arm.

He must just have arrived. The cold of the March night seemed to curl off him like frost. The sleeve of his jacket touched Bella's bare arm. It was like an electric shot to the heart. She flinched.

And said the first thing that came into her head.

'You're freezing! Did you walk here?'

'No. It just took some time to make anyone hear the bell. In the end I walked round to the kitchen.'

She was deeply suspicious. 'Why did you come?'

His smile became positively smug. 'Kosta broke his cuff-links for tomorrow. None of the rest of us wears them. So he called Tony to see if he could borrow. I'm just here collecting.'

Bella looked at him with the deepest suspicion. He leaned towards her and spoke so softly that she had to bend to catch the words.

'If I'd come to see you, I'd be standing outside your window, serenading right now.'

She felt rather breathless.

She did not let it show. Instead she looked down her nose at him and said in her most sarcastic tones, 'Oh, really?'

'I did think about it,' he said coolly. 'But I decided you'd probably want to get the wedding out of the way first.'

Bella's eyes narrowed. 'First?'

'Before we become lovers,' he explained.

She nearly fell off her perch.

He steadied her kindly. 'Careful.'

He did not remove his arm. It was like a steel bar.

She sent a quick look round the room. Tony's brandy was working its usual magic. There was an air of slightly dishevelled relaxation. Buttons were unbuttoned. One of Annis's godmothers had kicked off her shoes and had tucked her stockinged feet under her on the sofa as she explained her job to Annis's first headmaster.

Everyone was talking hard. No one was looking at Bella trapped in her corner. At least, not yet. They would all look pretty soon if she made a fuss about the hand at her waist.

She said for his ears only, 'We are not going to be lovers.'

'What makes you think that?' He sounded genuinely interested, damn him.

Bella set her teeth. 'I get a vote, don't I?'

That seemed to shock him. 'Of course.'

'Well, then,' she said triumphantly. 'I vote no.'

Gil smiled. She was so close, she could see the way the skin round his eyes crinkled with amusement.

'But I haven't started my campaign yet.'

She stood up sharply. Briefly his arm tightened, almost as a reflex. Then his arm fell and he leaned back among Lynda's stylish cushions and looked at her. Bella looked back, very steadily.

'No campaign,' she said.

For a moment he did not say anything. He was smiling but she had an uncomfortable feeling that it was pure surface. Underneath, he was not smiling at all.

As if to confirm her suspicion he said, quite gently, 'I'm afraid that's my decision.'

She was startled and it showed.

His smile grew. Real amusement this time. 'They usually do what you tell them, do they? The boys you play with?'

Bella did not know what to say.

'I can see a grown-up man will be a new experience.'

He did not touch her. He did not need to. She just stared at him, shaken.

Lynda came back with a small box in her hands. Gil lunged to his feet as she held it out to him.

'Thank you,' he said pocketing it. 'I'll see you tomorrow, Mrs Carew. Bella.' And with a nod he was gone.

'Such a kind man,' said Lynda, sighing.

Bella pointedly refrained from agreeing. She went back to Annis in a considerable temper.

But Annis was asleep. There was no one to explode to. Bella rescued the supper tray from its precarious position on the edge of the bed, restored a falling pillow and tiptoed out.

In the morning, of course, there was no time to talk about Gil or anything else except the wedding.

'I thought if we got married in the country, this wouldn't happen,' wailed Annis.

She was sitting in the old nursery, her hair in a sophisticated twist. The Victorian lace veil and gold filigree coronet had been anchored into place by a hairdresser who had just departed for his next bride. Under the bridal finery she wore faded jeans and a woollen shirt with paint stains on it. She looked pale.

'It always happens,' Bella assured her. She was a veteran bridesmaid. 'Two hundred guests or two thousand, it makes no difference. All it takes is one panicking bride, one fairy-tale dress and a woman about to become a mother-in-law.'

Annis shook her head. 'Lynda's been wonderful.'

'Sure, she has,' said Bella cordially. 'And she's driven you crazy. Goes with the territory.'

Annis gave a little choked laugh. 'Cynic.' But she looked more cheerful.

'Have a coffee and think about the honeymoon,' Bella advised.

But at the mention of coffee, Annis recoiled.

Bella was surprised. 'Up to you but I'm having some. We aren't allowed it once we climb into our finery.'

But still Annis shook her head.

Bella shrugged. 'OK. I'll check on Mother and be back.'

Predictably Lynda detained her in the kitchen. Two local cooks were setting out the tools of their trade while Lynda circled them like a nervous sheepdog.

'Sit, Mother,' said Bella at last, exasperated. 'They know what they're doing. Go and count buttonholes or something.'

She went back to Annis, muttering.

'When I get married, I'm not going to let her anywhere near the wedding. I couldn't take it.' She paused. 'Annis? Brain Box, are you there?'

A horrible sound came from the bathroom. Bella was taken aback.

'Annie?'

A wan face appeared round the bathroom door. The coronet was tilted drunkenly and the Victorian lace was knotted like a rag over her shoulder.

'Oh, boy, you do nerves in a big way,' said Bella, with sympathy.

She unscrewed a bottle of mineral water and poured a glass for Annis.

'Thank you,' said Annis palely. She sat down rather hard.

Bella took charge.

'OK. Countdown has started. I reckon you've got seventy-five minutes to sleep and still make it to the altar.'

Annis looked as if she was going to cry. 'But my hair—'

'I saw how he did it. I'll put your hair back up,' said Bella confidently. 'Just lose the crown for now, right? Go and lie down. I'll keep everyone at bay.'

She did. Eventually she also got herself into the glimmering blue robe that Annis had specified. Her hair was too sophisticated, she thought. She brushed it into a softer line and, with a slight grimace, fastened a spray of stephanotis above her ear with a diamond slide Tony had given her for her eighteenth birthday.

'There you are,' she told her reflection. 'Pretty and innocent. Stay that way.'

The trouble was, she didn't feel pretty and innocent. Gil de la Court had unsettled her. She wished she had crushed him last night. Failure to do so had left her oddly restless. She was resigned to having unwelcome emotions stirred up by this wedding. But she had never expected to walk down the aisle behind Annis seething with the frustrated desire to poke Gil de la Court in the eye.

'Pretty and innocent and sweet,' she said between her teeth. 'Got that? *Sweet!*'

She retrieved their bouquets, extracted Lynda from the kitchen again and went back upstairs to wake Annis. In the next forty minutes she flew upstairs and down, out into the courtyard to check on the waiting cars, into the conservatory to report the bride's progress to her father.

Finally Annis was buttoned into her creamy silks and Bella gave her headdress a last proprietorial tweak.

'Ready?'

Annis's eyes were very bright. 'Ready.'

Bella hugged her. 'You look wonderful.'

'Happiness is a great cosmetic,' said Annis, hugging her back. 'I'm so *lucky*.'

As the only bridesmaid, Bella got to ride to the church in solitary state. She took the opportunity to blow her nose hard. She did not want to risk dissolving into sentimental tears in the church.

She need not have worried. She was kept much too busy. They had not rehearsed the wedding and she was constantly on the alert, straightening Annis's skirt at one point, receiving her flowers at another. Eventually she was juggling two orders of service, two bouquets and a small girl who broke out of one of the guest pews to join the procession. She had no time to get weepy.

But there was a moment—

They had signed the register and turned to go down the aisle together. Annis looked up at her new husband. That was all. She just looked.

Of course, Kosta was one of the few men that tall Annis had ever had to tilt her head to look up to. Today, he looked stunningly handsome, with his midnight-black hair glinting in the rainbow light from the stained-glass windows. There was something gypsyish about him. Something not quite civilised. But then Bella saw the way the strange slanted eyes looked at his wife, as if she was treasure he could not quite believe. She saw what drew and held conservative Annis, thought Bella, shaken.

Kosta took Annis's hand and the organ burst into a blaze of gleeful chords. But for a moment it was as if the flower-filled church, the delighted friends and the pretty bridesmaid did not exist. They smiled straight into each other's eyes. It was an exchange of perfect understanding.

Bella felt a cold hand close round her heart. She had been pretending bravely but there was no pretence left now. She had never felt so lonely in her life. Kosta looked so *proud*.

Bella swallowed hard and followed them down the aisle with a smile that felt as if it had been welded in place.

From that moment on she flung herself into being the life and soul of the party.

She laughed when the March wind at the church door whipped her hair about her face, tipping the stephanotis over her eye at a drunken angle. She laughed harder when she slipped on the rain-washed flagstones and she had to grab the best man's arm to right herself. When a particularly vicious gust lifted Annis's veil into a balloon with a life of its own, it was Bella who wrestled with it, clowning for the cameras.

Oh, yes, she gave a brilliant performance. No one would have guessed that inside she was cold; and shivering; and frighteningly lonely. Flirting outrageously with the delighted best man, she looked in her element. A party girl and revelling in it.

'She gets better and better looking, doesn't she?' she overheard one of the godmothers say back at the house, as the champagne circulated before lunch. 'I never thought Annis would be the first to get married.'

'Oh, I don't know. Bella likes variety,' said someone else tolerantly.

'Should think so, gorgeous girl like that,' said the godmother's husband with enthusiasm. 'Plenty of time for her to settle down when she knows what she wants.'

Ouch, thought Bella.

She felt someone watching her and looked up. It was Gil de la Court. For a moment she was so relieved that it was not someone who had known her since she was a child, that she smiled brilliantly at him. He blinked.

Instantly she regretted it. She had told him not to mount a campaign in pursuit of her, after all. It was crazy to feel that he was her only ally in this gathering of friends and relations.

She turned away

Careful, she told herself. *Careful!*

She was standing next to a man she vaguely recognised. She smiled. Registered interest, eagerness. She smiled harder and, batting her eyelashes at him, leaned forward to listen with completely spurious attention. Out of the corner of her eye she saw Gil navigating his way round the godmothers towards her.

It was not a direct path. Lots of people wanted to talk to him. Their expressions varied between respect and downright wariness. He was courteous to all of them. But he did not stay long enough for more than a couple of sentences with any of them. And he did not deviate from his course.

'One thing at a time.' She remembered him saying that. Was she the one thing he was concentrating on today?

Longer than today, she reminded herself, thinking of the furnace of flowers he had sent her. Thinking, though she wished she could stop herself, of that hot kiss in the icy morning street. Much longer than today.

She turned her back so that, even out of the corner of her eye, she could no longer see him.

Even so, she knew when he reached her. He did not touch her. But she could feel him. What was more, she was almost certain he knew it.

'Hi,' he said, his voice unconvincingly solemn. 'Am I allowed to say you make a beautiful bridesmaid?'

He sounded heavily gallant and about ninety. For a moment, Bella was almost disappointed. But then she saw how she could turn it to her advantage. She could pretend that she did not know he was teasing her. She could take the laboured compliment at face value. She could use her party manners to play the game. And then maybe, just maybe, she would forget that surge of simple lust which he had so inexplicably uncorked when she was not looking.

So she turned and gave him her blandest smile. 'Thank you. How sweet of you.'

Her companion did not relish the interruption. Gil saw it. He held out his hand, smiling.

'Gilbert de la Court. Friend of the bride. And the bride's sister.'

How did he manage to make it sound as if owned her, thought Bella, fuming. Or did he? Was it just her own over-sensitivity to him at work again?

Her companion was impressed. His resistance to the interruption evaporated.

'De la Court. Of course. Saw you on the news last night. I hear that your launch has set a new record.'

'The markets have been kind to Watifdotcom,' said Gil.

Bella looked at him narrowly. It sounded like a piece of learned dialogue. As soon as they got rid of her admirer, she accused him of it.

'Of course,' he said coolly.

'You have a scriptwriter for your party conversation?' She was outraged.

His eyes narrowed. 'Why not?'

'How much of what you said to me came from your resident joke writer?'

'Ah,' he said enlightened. 'You like your men spontaneous.'

'Of course I—' She stopped dead, realising too late the trap she had fallen into. 'You are not one of *my men*.'

'So I should hope.'

That disconcerted her. 'What?'

'I just hate to be one of a crowd.'

He was teasing again. His eyes laughed down at her. But there was something in their expression that was not teasing at all.

'You—' But she looked into his eyes and felt what she was going to say slip away from her. 'I—I mean—'

Hopeless! Bella felt hot and confused. Her eyes fell.

It was crazy. She was as off balance as a teenager with her first love. Yet she was a woman, a sophisticated, popular women. What was more, she knew how to play the delicate game of flirtation. She had an instinct for it, always had had. Her mother said she had been born with it.

So what was happening to her? She had had more boyfriends than she could remember. Some of them had been major heartthrobs, too. None of them had ever made her look away and stammer like a schoolgirl.

It was not even as if she was really interested in him. She could not be.

All right, there had been that sizzling kiss. But it was easy enough to account for, if she thought about it. She had been lonely in New York. Then Annis's unexpected arrival had thrown her off balance. It had reminded her, heaven help her, of everything from which she had been running so hard to escape. The kiss had been fuelled by a lot that had nothing to do with Gil de la Court—the heady excitement of those Latin rhythms, the strange unreality of the city night, savage loneliness, exile…

And lust, thought Bella, with lacerating truth. *Don't forget lust.*

She remembered the moment when she had almost let him come up to her apartment. She felt as if she was suffocating.

She said, in pure reflex, 'Don't do this.'

It was not much above a whisper. But there was no doubting her passionate sincerity.

Gil's eyes flickered. 'What's wrong?' he said, not teasing any more.

She was shocked into complete honesty.

'I'm already in love,' she said in a harsh undertone. 'I wish I wasn't but there's no point in pretending.'

His face stilled. He said nothing. Bella wondered if he had understood.

'Don't waste your time,' she said painfully. 'There's only room for one.'

Still he said nothing. For some reason, quite suddenly, she wanted to cry.

'Weddings!' she said furiously. 'Turn everyone into a fountain. Excuse me—'

She fled.

From then on she whirled through the party like a butterfly on speed. Even when Lynda eventually managed to get her guests seated in the marquee that had been attached to the conservatory, Bella hardly sat still for a minute. She was continually jumping up: to kiss an old friend here; to fetch a clean glass there; to play pat-a-cake games with a grizzling four-year-old so that the exhausted parents could eat one course in peace; to laugh and joke—and never, ever, look in Gil de la Court's direction. By the time the cake was brought in for its ceremonial dismemberment, she felt ready to collapse with sheer exhaustion.

And she was not the only one, by the looks of it. Annis was looking dreadfully pale again. She laughed for the cameras, and she and Kosta held the knife. But, as they cut into the cake, Bella was fairly certain that it was only his hand over hers that stopped Annis from shaking pitiably. What on earth was wrong? Was she ill?

All thought of her own problems fled. As soon as the cake was taken away to be sliced for the guests, she saw Annis slide her hand out of Kosta's. She murmured something in his ear and slipped away. Bella put down her untasted champagne and followed.

She caught up with Annis in her bedroom. She was sitting in the window seat, her cheek against the glass and her eyes closed. She looked green.

'Annie!' exclaimed Bella, shocked.

Annis didn't open her eyes. 'It's all right. It doesn't last. I'll be right as rain in two ticks.'

Quite suddenly Bella understood a lot of things: the way Annis had snapped last night; her tiredness; this morning's sickness. Maybe that illness in New York that had sent her off to Hombre y Mujer with no companions but the Japanese tourists.

'It's not nerves, is it?' she said, almost inaudibly.

Annis shook her head, eyes still closed.

'I see.'

Bella felt numb.

She got Annis some water and retreated.

'Is there anything I can do?' She could hear the constraint in her voice.

Annis gave a wry smile. 'Maybe babysitting in the fullness of time.' She opened her eyes. 'Don't look so worried, Bella Bug. It really does pass.'

'So I've heard.' Bella tried to smile. This was a nightmare. 'Do you want anything?'

Annis shook her head. 'Just rest. That usually does it.'

'Then, I'll leave you.'

Bella went.

It felt like an escape. She was shaking. She hadn't felt like this since she'd first realised that

Annis was in love with Kosta and he with her. Since she'd first known that, all her bright hopes had come crashing down without anyone even noticing.

She took refuge in her stepfather's study. It was out of bounds to the guests and the caterers alike. Besides it contained the big-wing chair she had hidden in as a child when Tony had taught her to play hide-and-seek.

She sank back into it, pulling up her knees and hugging them. No one just looking in would have known there was anyone in the room at all.

What's wrong with me, she thought. *Why should I care that Annis and Kosta are going to have a baby? I lost Kosta months ago. Heck, I never had him. The moment he clapped eyes on Annis I lost any chance I ever had with him. The baby makes no difference.*

And yet…

She had thought she could not feel lonelier. It seemed she was wrong.

Across the courtyard, the wedding party laughed and chatted and toasted everyone concerned. Bella knew she would have to go back and join in soon. But she did not move.

I'm all out of revelry, she thought.

The door opened. Bella held her breath. She knew she was invisible in the great chair. All she had to do was sit still as a mouse and the intruder would go away.

Only he didn't. He closed the door behind him and just stood there quietly, waiting.

She stood it as long as she could. Then she catapulted out of the chair to face him.

'What?' she flung at him.

'Thought so,' said Gil de la Court with satisfaction.

'OK, so you found me. Big deal.'

Bella shook out her skirts. The stuff glinted like a peacock's tail, jade and emerald and turquoise. With a bit of luck, among all that flamboyant colour, no one would notice how she had creased it.

He ignored her fussing with her dress.

'Why are you hiding?'

'I'm not any more,' she pointed out.

'But you were.' It was not a question.

She shrugged. 'I've been doing my cabaret act for hours. I needed a break.'

'I noticed.'

'What?'

'The all singing, all dancing Bella show,' he said drily.

She was taken aback. 'What do you mean?'

'Well, who is the star of today's performance?'

Her chin came up at that. The abrupt movement dislodged her headdress. The stephanotis flopped annoyingly over her brow. She pushed it back with an impatient hand.

'So?'

'Wasn't there supposed to be a bride around somewhere?'

Bella winced. 'Annis isn't feeling well.'

He snapped his fingers. 'Of course. That must be it.'

She was suddenly, gloriously angry. She gave him a glittering smile that was a hundred and ten per cent fury.

'No, of course that isn't it,' she said affably. 'You know what they say about stepsisters. Well, here I am to prove it. Upstaging Annis at her own wedding.'

His brows twitched together.

She remembered what Lynda had said. That he had been more than halfway in love with Annis. It looked as if her mother was right. In which case why had he been chasing Bella so hard ever since New York? It added fuel to a fire that was already burning quite brightly.

'How clever of you to find me out. You must be really pleased with yourself.'

The damned flower fell over her face again. She dashed it away with an unsteady hand. The waxy bloom flew straight across the room as if she had thrown it. He caught it instinctively.

'My, what fast reflexes you have,' said Bella. She made it sound like an insult and was glad. She knew how close she was to tears. And she was not going to cry in front of this man. She was *not*. Blinking furiously, she made to barge past him.

'Fast enough,' he said, suddenly grim.

He'd caught her so neatly. He'd let her own impetus take her into his arms. Hard. And before she could catch her breath or her balance he was kissing her.

Bella's roar of outrage was muffled by his mouth. This was not like the icy morning kiss. He was not nearly so controlled this time. In fact, she was not sure that he was controlled at all. His arms were like iron but she could feel little tremors in his hands, and under his ribs, like a volcano about to erupt. And his arousal was unmistakeable.

She had a moment of primitive panic at that raw physicality.

And then civilisation reasserted itself. For both of them, fortunately.

He let her go. He was rather pale and his mouth was a taut line.

'Not here,' he said curtly.

'Not—' Bella looked at him speechlessly. 'What do you mean by that?'

The look he gave her was deeply ironic.

She did not pretend to misunderstand him. 'Forget it.'

His eyes were hard. 'Don't think I can,' he said with devastating honesty. 'Can you?'

No said something inside her, something very deep and old, something she had never heard before.

Bella gave him a horrified look.

Before she could speak, he said, 'I know you think you're in love with someone else. Well, where is he? If he was worth your loyalty, he would be here with you today, wouldn't he?'

She shook her head with a despairing laugh.

'Does he know you, like I know you?'

'You don't understand.'

'Yes, I do. I've watched you all day.'

Her throat was so full, she could hardly speak. 'Gil—'

'You make a beautiful bridesmaid. You do a great job as the daughter of the manor. Only I'd rather have Tina the Tango Dancer. Where did she go, Bella?'

He touched the side of her face with clumsy, tentative fingers. It was too much. A tear brimmed over. She felt it trickle down her cheek. He must have seen it too but he did not look away.

'All that fire. All that passion,' he said. 'And look at you now. What do I have to do to get her back, my Tina?'

The tears were falling fast now. She had to work hard keeping her eyes wide open to abate them enough to be able to see.

'Stop it,' she shouted. 'Just stop it. You just don't understand. Nobody understands.'

This time she got past him before he could stop her. She thought he called her name but she didn't care. She banged the door on him.

It took her some time to cool down. Even longer to splash water on her face to get rid of the tell-tale signs of tears. After that she repaired her make-up and did what she could with her hair. Still, New York expertise told, and when she went back to join the party she knew she looked good.

Which was just as well because the first person she walked into was her new brother-in-law.

'Hi, gorgeous,' said Kosta.

Of course, he had never taken her seriously, thought Bella. In an odd way, that made the memories easier.

'Hi, yourself,' she said, with a friendly smile.

She gave him a hug that she convinced herself was sisterly. It was certainly enthusiastic enough to have come from an exuberant baby sister. That was what it would have looked like to the other guests. Maybe that was what it felt like to Kosta. That was certainly the way he had treated her ever since he had got engaged to Annis. It was as if that night, the dark secret never very far below the surface of her memory, had never happened.

He hugged her back. 'Where's my beautiful wife?'

'Resting.'

'Sick, eh?' He pulled a face. 'She's having a bad time, poor love. And today has been a strain. I told her we should pull out of the wedding. Run away to sea and get married in Tahiti. But she didn't want to disappoint Lynda.'

Bella smiled without constraint for the first time for hours. 'That's my Annis.'

'Yeah. That tender heart is going to take some living up to,' said Kosta with feeling.

'You'll manage it.'

He squeezed her shoulders. 'You're a good friend.'

'I try,' said Bella drily.

'*And* a stunner. I think you've knocked poor old Gil for six. He kept asking about you last night.'

'Did he?' said Bella. The constraint was back again with a vengeance.

'So I told him you were a heartbreaker and supplied a list of men who'd bear me out,' said Kosta cheerfully.

'Thank you.'

'Didn't look as if it was going to make any difference.'

Well, it wouldn't. Not to a man who thought he knew her better than anyone in her life had ever known her on the strength of one dance, one car journey and two kisses.

And could just possibly be right.

The thought stopped her dead in her tracks.

Right? *Right?*

But surely the only man who knew her was the one who knew her terrible secret? The man who had been there and had seen it. The man who had caused it. The man who, very kindly, very chivalrously, had turned her down and had sent her away.

Except that, as he'd proved every time they'd met, as he had just proved again, he didn't know her at all. Oh, he knew what happened. But he didn't know what it had meant. Not at the time. Not since. He probably thought she behaved like that with every man who happened to take her fancy. If he thought about it at all.

Bella gave a strangled laugh. 'The problem with weddings is they make people want to pair everyone else off too.'

'You could be right,' said Kosta equably. 'So you think Gil's got wedding fever, do you?'

No, she didn't. There had been no wedding to infect him that icy night in New York. But she was not telling anyone else that. She was scarcely even admitting it to herself.

'Yes,' she said, lying through her teeth.

Kosta laughed. 'Whatever you say.' He looked at his watch. 'I ought to go and change if we're going to do the ceremonial departure. I wish we didn't have to come back for the dance. The sooner I get Annis out of this madhouse and onto a nice warm beach the better.'

'Sounds like heaven,' said Bella, meaning it.

'Then, you ought to string Gil along for a bit. He's got his very own place on a Greek island. You could get the holiday of a lifetime out of him before you give him his cards.'

'I'll bear it in mind,' she said with irony.

'Do that. He's due for a bit of fun. He works too hard, Annis says. And he had his heart broken by the wrong woman.'

Bella was taken aback, in the light of Lynda's account of Gil's romantic history.

'Did Annis tell you that?' she asked cautiously.

'No.' He was not very interested. 'I forget who told me. She was someone he worked with, I think. His lost lady, I mean.'

She could just have become your wife, thought Bella. In spite of herself, she felt a touch of fellow-feeling for Gil de la Court.

She still avoided him for the rest of the afternoon. Quite possibly he was trying to avoid her too. She certainly did not see him again until Annis came downstairs hand in hand with Kosta, ready to be waved off in the car to which assorted boots, bottles and jocular notices had been attached.

Annis was looking as radiant as a bride ought to now. Her rest had restored her colour. And she leaned against Kosta's shoulder with absolute confidence. Bella felt that treacherous little hand squeeze her heart again. She held back as the guests all surged forward half carrying Annis and Kosta to the waiting car.

A voice in her ear said, 'What are you doing now?'

She did not look round. She said evenly, 'Waving goodbye to my sister.'

'And then?'

Quite suddenly she knew she couldn't take any more. The smart evening dress would stay in her suitcase. The dance would have to take place without her.

'Getting out of the bridesmaid's uniform and heading back to London,' she said with resolution.

'I'll drive you.'

'But the dance—'

Gil was obstinate. 'I drove you down. I'll drive you back.'

'That's not necessary.'

'Oh, yes, it is. You have no idea how necessary.'

'There's no point. We've got nothing to talk about.'

'We agree on something, then,' he said, startling her into looking round at him.

Only then there was a concerted rush for the car. As Bella looked, distracted, a laughing Annis staggered under the onslaught. At once, Kosta swung an arm round her, shielding her with his body.

'The bouquet,' someone shouted. 'Throw the bouquet.'

Annis had obviously brought it downstairs with her for that express purpose. She scanned the crowd, clearly looking for someone.

Bella had a sudden and horrible premonition.

'No,' she said under her breath. 'Oh, no, please.'

But Annis had seen her. She looked momentarily disconcerted to find her sister right at the back of the laughing group. She said something to Kosta. He bent his head, then looked up at where Bella stood. A broad smile dawned.

He took the bouquet from Annis and swung his arm a couple of times experimentally.

How could he, thought Bella, knowing what he was going to do and not quite believing it. How *could* he?

He whirled the bouquet in a powerful over-arm throw. It arced high over the leaping crowd and hit Bella full in the face. She tried to avoid it but there was nothing she could do. She staggered. She might even have fallen if Gil had not steadied her, catching the bouquet one-handed as it recoiled.

A cheer went up.

He grinned waving the bouquet above his head. 'My luck's changed.'

Bella pretended that the shock in her eyes came from a scratch from one of the wired freesias. Gil gave her a handkerchief. She managed to wipe her eyes and blow her nose under the guise of dabbing at some non-existent wound.

The guests turned back to Annis and Kosta and she breathed again. But she was still reverberating like a tuning fork.

Kosta at the wheel, the car did a lap of honour. As it passed, Bella saw Annis take Kosta's hand and put it on her stomach. They exchanged a look of affectionate complicity. And total trust. And love.

For a moment Bella could hardly breathe.

Alone, she thought. *I'm alone. I'll always be alone. He doesn't remember because he never noticed.*

And beside her was Gil de la Court who had noticed all right.

She turned to him, little tremors still running through her, but her head high.

'OK.'

'What?'

'You can give me that lift,' said Bella. Her smile glittered. She was offering a lot more than a lift and she could see that he knew it. 'As soon as you like.'

CHAPTER SEVEN

IT WAS surprisingly easy to get away. Bella expected a protest from Lynda but it did not come.

'Don't blame you,' said Tony Carew, holding his wife's hand firmly. 'The young men will be disappointed but we'll just tell them you had a plane to catch.'

So she changed quickly into trousers and a soft cashmere sweater in tabby-cat colours and kissed a few selected guests goodbye, smiling carefully.

'Your turn next,' said one of the godmothers, hugging her.

The smile stayed in place. 'Sure.'

'I'll call you when I come to New York,' said the man she had flirted with before lunch.

'Sure.'

'Don't *want* you to go,' said the child she had played pat-a-cake with.

Bella gave him a quick, grateful hug.

Gil put her bag in his car. Bella kissed her parents. Tony mussed her hair, as he'd used to do when she went back to school as a child. Then Lynda linked an arm in his and Bella got into the car. As they drove off, Tony and Lynda waved. By that time they were hand in hand and Bella's mouth ached with smiling.

Gil looked in the driving mirror as he swirled the car into the shadow of the great laurel hedge and away down the drive.

'You seem very close.'

'They're very close.' In spite of herself she sounded desolate. She pulled herself together. 'I mean, we all are. Close, I mean.'

He sent her a quick look.

'You get on well with your stepfather, don't you?'

'Always.'

'Do you still see your real father?'

Bella was surprised into telling the truth. Something she did not often do about Micky Spence.

'Tony is my real father. The other was just a biological accident.'

Gil digested this. 'I'll take that as a no, shall I?'

She shrugged. What did it matter, after all? She might as well tell him the truth. She was going back to New York tomorrow. After today she would probably never see him again.

'He was a classic. Good-looking kid with a guitar wants to be a rock star. He trailed mum around all over Europe, looking for the breaks.

She used to work at all sorts of casual jobs, just to keep us going. She can pour drinks in five languages, do you know that? He used to spend our money on cutting terrible discs.'

'You remember him?'

'Sort of.' She paused. Then, quite suddenly, it burst out of her. 'And the fights. And the parties. Micky used to bring home guys from the clubs where he was playing. They would jam for the rest of the night. Mother and I would be huddled in a corner trying to sleep. We never had more than one room. He frightened me.' She glanced at him sideways. 'Have I shocked you?'

There was a pause. Then he said carefully, 'Did you want to shock me?'

She made an unusually clumsy gesture. 'I've never told anyone that. Not even my mother.'

He drew a sharp breath.

Bella did not notice. 'I never thought I would tell anyone,' she said, more than half to herself. 'I guess it was waiting to come out and today just pulled the plug. *Bloody* weddings.'

It was dark and rain thundered on the roof. Trees bent in the wind. The car was luxuriously heated but she shivered all the same.

'What happened to him?'

'He ran out on us,' she said in a hard voice. 'When Tony wanted to marry my mother, they had a really hard job to track him down to give her a divorce.'

'But he did.'

'Oh, yes. Unloading the wife and child was all Micky ever wanted to do as long as I knew him.'

'And now?'

She shrugged again. 'He was running the cabaret in some beach resort hotel the last I heard. That would suit him. He thinks life is one long party.'

'Sounds like you haven't forgiven him.'

'Forgiven him?' she said jeeringly. 'What have I got to forgive? I'm just like him.'

Gil didn't answer for a moment. Then he said in a carefully neutral voice, 'You're musical?'

It was so unexpected it startled a choke of laughter out of Bella.

'No,' she allowed grudgingly.

'Then in what respect do you resemble him?'

'You sound like a professor,' she complained. She primmed up her lips and mocked his precise accent, echoing his words. '"In what respect—?" Pff!'

'I have been a professor in my time,' he said, unoffended. 'If Watifdotcom goes down the tubes, it's back to teaching for me. I've even held on to the website I set up when I was an academic, so my colleagues don't forget me.'

'Sensible,' said Bella in a depressed voice.

Gil sent her a shrewd look. 'OK, come on, give. What makes you like this guitar-playing hellion?'

'I'm a party girl,' she said, goaded.

'Ah.'

'Don't you believe me? You should have listened to the guests back there. "Give twenty reasons why Bella is not a marriageable proposition."' She laughed again, but there was an edge to her laughter. It mocked herself, not kindly.

He did not answer. He seemed to be deep in thought.

Then he said, 'Do you want to be?'

'What?'

'A marriageable proposition. Do you want to be married?'

But she skittered away from answering that one.

'Who knows?' She shivered again, looking out at the darkness of the rural lane. The wind sounded like a banshee and the trees looked tortured. 'This is a terrible night.'

A small lake of water had accumulated at the side of the road. He did not see it until they were nearly in it. A tidal wave splashed Bella's window and she jumped. He slewed out into the middle of the road at once.

'Damn.'

'What?'

'Driving without proper concentration. You're a distraction, Bella Carew.'

'Thank you,' she said. She sounded forlorn, even to her own ears.

He sent her another of those quick, shrewd glances. Bella felt it, even though she was not looking at him. Her body was taut as a spring.

'It's a compliment.'

'Sure.'

'It is, believe me. Takes a lot to distract me. I'm famed for my concentration.'

'Then, I'm flattered,' she said, politely disbelieving.

He gave an exasperated sigh. But at that point a car came round a curve in the road towards them, its headlights blazing, and he had to divert all his attention to the road.

'Either this road surface is exceptionally uneven or that car is flashing us,' he remarked. He slowed the car to a crawl.

The approaching vehicle slowed too. As they came abreast, the driver stopped and lowered his window.

'Sit back,' said Gil, pressing the switch to slide the driver's window down.

At once the cool, damp air filled the car. Driving rain turned the shoulder of his jacket black as he leaned out.

'Tree down,' yelled the other driver. 'Road's blocked. And the river broke its banks. The back road is under three feet of water. We're stuck until they clear it. I'm going home.'

'Thanks.'

Gil raised the window and sat back, looking at Bella.

'Want to go back?'

She thought of the dance. All that unbridled merriment.

'No.'

He did not argue but he said, 'Interesting choice for a party girl.'

He thought for a bit, then put the car in gear and turned it round neatly in the middle of the dark road.

'I said I didn't want to go back.' Her voice rose.

'Relax. I know a place we can stay round here. I played cricket in the village once. The pub has rooms. All I've got to do is find it.'

'Oh.'

He didn't speak again until suddenly there were intermittent street lamps. One house, two, then a cluster of workman's cottages behind densely planted gardens. And then the road curved, and the hedgerows and houses gave way to a village green like a lake of blackness in the prevailing dark.

'There,' said Gil with satisfaction.

The rain lashed across the windscreen blindingly. On the far side of the green, lights flickered as a creeper blew back and forth across their welcoming warmth. The pub sign creaked on its hinges, flying as high as a six-year-old on a swing.

Bella shivered. 'It looks like the end of the world.'

'Nonsense,' said Gil bracingly. 'The place is pure Pickwick. You'll feel better when you're out of the storm.'

He was right.

Inside there were two blazing fires, a dart's match in one bar, a lively debate about the spring horticultural show in the other. No one paid any attention to the storm raging outside. But they made room for Bella by the fire while Gil negotiated accommodation. Bella pushed wet hair out of her eyes and held out her hands to the flames.

'Come far?' said one of the daffodil growers kindly.

Bella looked across the room. Gil was deep in conversation with the landlord. Firelight glinted off his hair. He looked as timeless as the copper jugs and polished wood all around him. Timeless and *strong*. Some sleeping thing turned over inside her.

The daffodil grower repeated his question.

'Far?' echoed Bella.

In the flickering light she saw his profile suddenly illuminated: high, autocratic nose; deep, deep eyes; passionate mouth… Why had she forgotten how she'd responded to that Regency-rake mouth?

He must have felt her eyes on him. He looked up. Bella felt the world lurch. The sleeping thing was asleep no longer. Suddenly she was furnace-hot.

He looked away. The landlord said something. Gil leaned forward, concentrating. But she could see the way his chest rose and fell. She did not think she was the only one who felt the heat.

'Oh, yes,' she said softly to the daffodil grower, 'I've come a long, long way.'

Gil came back to her. His breathing was under control now. He smiled at her companion and slipped easily into the commonplace of practicalities. But she knew him now. Everyone else in the room might be oblivious but Bella had seen the little flame in his eyes. She knew that, under the cool control, he was shaking. Because she was too.

'They've got room for us. Probably a bit makeshift. It's early in the season for tourists, so they weren't really prepared. I said that would be all right.'

Bella listened carefully. He did not say they had to share a room. He did not say that they didn't. Maybe she had a choice. Did she want a choice?

She felt bewildered and off balance, as if she had suddenly found herself on the wrong aeroplane: she did not know where she was going but it was not possible to get off until she got there. It might be interesting. It might be terrifying. She had no way of knowing. Or how she was going to find her way back.

She swallowed. 'Yes. That's fine.' Her voice didn't sound like her own.

He said her name. His voice was so low, she did not think anyone else could hear. It seemed to reach right into her. She gave a low laugh, half excitement, half pure panic. Not that she would have admitted it. Party girls didn't panic.

She said sedately for the others to hear, 'Can you find out if there's any chance of food?'

'I knew you'd ask that.'

'Really?' She smiled into his eyes and watched them darken with desire. It seemed there were two conversations going on here. But only one was in words. 'Why?' she said, making him focus on the audible one.

'You didn't eat a thing at lunch. I saw you push the food all around your plate.'

'You *watched* me?' She was not sure how she felt about that. It was slightly alarming to feel that she had been under surveillance and had not known it.

'All the time. I nearly killed that kid with the clapping game.'

'What? Why?'

'He had you and I wanted you.'

She was breathing unevenly. 'You could have come and joined us.'

'No I couldn't.' His voice dropped. 'I wanted you to myself.'

Bella swallowed. He saw it and smiled. A little shiver ran through her, like the ripple on a lake before a storm.

Gil saw that too. She knew he saw it. But he carried on the verbal conversation as if nothing had happened. 'They can do something simple. Home-made soup. Something grilled.' His eyes caressed her.

Bella was suddenly conscious of breathing. It didn't seem to be as easy as it was supposed to be.

'Fine,' she said with an effort.

'So what would you like?'

She couldn't think about food. She couldn't *think*.

'You choose,' she said, impatient with herself.

'Do you trust me?'

There was a sharp little silence. Bella gave herself a mental shake.

'We are still talking about food, right?'

He looked innocent. 'What else?'

Damn, but he was good at this.

She said drily, 'Do a lot of this, do you?'

'That's a loaded question.' His eyes, she found, were very intent. 'Do you?'

Ouch!

'Soup,' she said loudly. 'I'm not very hungry.'

He did not push it. But she could see from the speculative look in his eye that he was not going to let it rest. There was a question there that he wanted to know the answer to. And, from what she had seen of Gil de la Court, he got all the answers he wanted. Eventually.

The food was served in an alcove in the dining room which was specially opened up for their convenience. The proprietor lit candles, brought soup and crusty bread and retreated to the bar, closing the door behind him.

Alone in the candlelight they looked at each other.

Gil said softly, 'Your eyes are blue. I couldn't remember.'

Bella felt inexplicably shy. Her eyes fell. She stirred the thick broth absorbedly.

'Did you tell them to leave us alone?'

Even though she wasn't looking at him, she could feel his amusement.

'No.'

'Then, why?'

'I imagine because they weren't expecting guests and they've got a couple of rooms to make up.'

She was so startled, she forgot that she wasn't looking at him.

'A couple?'

He held her eyes steadily. 'Yes.'

'But I—'

He leaned forward and took her hand.

'Bella, listen to me.'

She could not believe it. 'You don't want me,' she said numbly.

'Of course I want you.'

She shook her head. 'More games,' she said almost to herself.

His hand tightened over her fingers.

'No. *Listen.* This is important.'

She was so humiliated she hardly heard him. He drummed their clasped hands on the table.

'Look at me.'

It would be a total defeat if she didn't. Fighting to keep her expression under control, Bella raised her head.

'Oh, my love,' he said on a shocked breath. Then, rapidly, he went on, 'I want you all right. Of course I do. I want you to sleep with me. I hope you will. But there's a force ten gale out there and you've had a hell of a day. I'm not sure *you* know what *you* want. Or whether what you wanted when we left the party is the same as you will want an hour from now.'

Bella stared.

He raised her hand. Still holding her eyes he brushed his mouth gently across her knuckles. It was nowhere near a kiss. But it started a trembling deep inside her, more insistent than any kiss she had ever known.

'I just want you to be clear. You have a choice,' he said simply. 'You will go on having a choice.'

She was shaken to the core.

But Gil picked up his spoon and began to drink his soup as if nothing very momentous had happened. He kept hold of her hand though.

Eventually Bella pulled herself together enough to say, 'You must think I'm an awful fool.'

He looked faintly surprised. 'No. Why?'

'Well—' she was floundering '—having to spell it out like that.'

'Spell it out?' For a moment he was blank. Then he smiled, shaking his head. 'Oh, the bedrooms. That's for my benefit, not yours. I'm sure you don't need things spelled out. It's me. I'm not what you call good at this sort of thing.'

Bella forgot her embarrassment—and that steady inner trembling—in sheer fascination. 'Are you trying to tell me you don't date?'

He was rueful. 'That's one way of putting it.'

'How would you put it, then?'

'I'd say I have a general blind spot when it comes to human nature.'

Bella leaned forward and scanned his expression. He looked back openly enough but she had the impression that, for all his matter-of-fact tone, this was a sensitive subject. That he *minded*.

She said quite gently, 'Want to tell me about it?'

'What's to tell?' He shrugged. 'I was a fully classified genius before I was ten. There's a certain sort of education that goes along with being a genius. It doesn't include the signs that ordinary people take for granted.'

Bella was bewildered. 'Signs? What signs?'

He looked round for inspiration. 'Oh, stuff like candlelight and romance. By the time they're adolescent, most people know there's a connection. People like you, for example. I had to be told.' And, as she still stared, he said in exasperation, 'I suppose I mean non-verbal indicators.'

Bella gave a gulp of startled laughter. 'Non-verbal—! What on earth is a non-verbal indicator?'

'Dancing. Kissing.' He listed them, concentrating. 'Sex.'

She choked on her soup.

'Sex?' She used his own words back to him. 'You have a blind spot when it comes to sex?' She looked at that passionate mouth and was justifiably incredulous.

'As a tool of communication, yes.' He was dispassionate, dry as the professor he'd said he had been.

'I don't believe this,' Bella muttered.

He shrugged.

'It's not supposed to be a tool for anything. It's supposed to be fun.'

'Is it?'

'Hey, lighten up.' She tipped her head on one side and batted her eyelashes at him, deliberately exaggerated. 'See?'

Gil surveyed her, unmoving, for a moment. Then he sighed.

Bella stopped batting her eyelashes, disgruntled. 'What?'

'You don't have to perform for me,' he said drily. 'I respond to all the usual stimuli.'

'Oh!' She flushed furiously.

'I'm just not good at knowing what it all means. Really means.'

She pressed her hands to her hot cheeks. How could he make her feel so small? Without even trying, it seemed.

He said again, quietly, 'Look at me Bella.'

Reluctantly she did. Her flush was taking a long time to subside. How long had it been since she blushed like that? Not since she was a teenager, anyway.

Gil said levelly, 'Everyone thinks I'm brilliant. In some ways it's true. I can do sums—see pathways—very quickly. It's a useable talent in this day and age. I've built a business on it and I will go on building. But it's no guide to human nature.'

She scanned his face. This was obviously important to him. But—

'I don't understand,' Bella said honestly.

He sighed. 'Let me give you an example. I have a team that depends on me to go on building that business. Friends, most of them. And I nearly blew it because I didn't see what was going on under my nose.'

She struggled to translate and failed.

'You were having an affair with someone you worked with?'

'No. No, these weren't sexual signs. This was other sorts of behaviour. But it was there, plain for anyone to see who was a fully paid-up member of the human race. Annis was. I wasn't.'

Bella stared.

He moved the cutlery on the table into a precise pattern. 'I hear what people say. I just don't know what they mean.' His smile was painful. 'I suppose I need a translator. Someone like you.'

'Like *me*?'

'You seem to have the twenty-first century sussed,' Gil pointed out.

'You're joking, right?'

He was puzzled. She could see it. 'No.'

'But I'm a walking disaster.'

He laughed, his eyes suddenly warm. 'I don't buy that. A tango-dancing disaster, maybe.'

Bella shivered. 'Oh, I can get dressed up in my party gear and dazzle the world. Doesn't stop me making a complete prat of myself.'

Remembering just how complete a prat, her whole body flinched.

Gil's dark eyes narrowed. 'You are talking about a specific instance, aren't you? Want to tell me?'

Bella swallowed, shaking her head. She could still hardly bear to remember that shaming scene. Every time it came into her mind, she recoiled, wincing. She was not ready to tell anyone else about it. Not even someone who thought he had his own disasters.

'I—can't—' she said, with difficulty.

He saw her distress. 'It can't be that bad.'

'Oh, yes, it can,' said Bella, pulling herself together. 'I know you think I'm—what was it you called me in New York?—a girl who likes to live on the edge?'

'Yes,' he said. A ghost of a smile played about that voluptuary's mouth. 'Are you trying to tell me I was wrong?'

'Oh, no, you were right,' she said with bitter self-mockery. 'Live on the edge and sometimes you fall off. I did.'

He digested that.

'It doesn't show,' he said at last.

Bella shrugged. 'So I'm a good liar.'

He banged his fist down on the table, making the cutlery sing and Bella jump.

'That's exactly what I'm talking about.'

She stared. 'I don't follow.'

'I can read men,' he said impatiently. 'Well, most of them. But women hide and shift and tell half-truths. I get them wrong every time.' He sounded as if he really despised himself.

Bella found she could not bear it.

'You didn't,' she said loudly, 'get me wrong.'

It was his turn to stare. 'What?'

Again she quoted him. '"I'm not sure you know what you want. You've had a hell of day."' She smiled painfully. 'How many other people do you think noticed me having a hell of a day? I was doing the bridesmaid-as-cheer-leader bit. And, as you say, I'm good at it. Even my mother didn't see that I was desperate to escape.'

Gil's eyes widened. In the candlelight they were brown velvet shot with gold. Suddenly he was not looking inwards, castigating himself, he was looking at her, really looking at her. She saw his eyes soften, turn warm and melting. She began to feel breathless.

Suddenly speech was difficult. 'But you saw it,' she managed.

There was complete silence.

This time it was Bella who took his hand.

'Thank you for the second room,' she said quietly. 'But it won't be needed.'

The storm went on rising. Rain lashed against the windows like automatic-weapons fire. The old building seemed to shudder at the wind. And then the lights went out.

'Just as well I lit the fires in your rooms,' said the owner, coming in with more candles. 'The central heating will be out till morning now. We emptied the coffee machine into a couple of Thermos flasks, though, so you don't have to go without coffee.'

Bella's fingers twitched in his, turned and clasped strongly.

Gil took up the message, smooth as a runner handed a baton.

'No coffee, thank you. We'll go up now.'

'Fine. I'll show you the way.'

She gave them a candle each and raised her own branch high to illumine the uneven wooden stairs. Bella did not let go of Gil's hand as they followed.

The rooms were next door to each other, off a creaking corridor. In spite of the log fires, both were chilly.

'Sorry about that,' said the owner. 'Whoever takes the four-poster can pull the curtains round it. That generally keeps the heat in.'

She said goodnight.

Left alone, they looked at each other. Then Gil took Bella's candle from her. He put both candles down carefully.

She gave a little laugh, half excitement, half embarrassment.

Embarrassment? Me? Sophisticate and world-class party girl? How can I be embarrassed?

But she was. All she wanted was to be in his arms. And she did not know how to get there.

It was crazy. All she had to do was walk over to him, take his face in her hands and kiss that rake's mouth until he lost control. Then they would be fine.

But something she had not felt before staked her to the spot. Something that said, *this is too important to get it wrong*. Something that said, *if you take charge here, you've blown it.* Something that said, *Help!*

And Gil—Gil who'd said he had a blind spot about sex and got women wrong—rescued her.

He said, 'Looks like we're going to have to keep each other warm.' He sounded amused. And a lot more.

Bella, cool-hearted sophisticate and twenty-first century guru, trembled.

'Come here?' That didn't sound amused at all. It sounded deadly serious. But it was still a question. It seemed that, even now, he was reminding her that she still had a choice.

So in the end it was quite easy to walk into his arms, after all.

* * *

Later, when the candles had guttered and the tree outside was rattling its leaves against the old leaded window, Bella lay in his arms, staring at the shadows the firelight set dancing. She cradled his hand where it cupped her breast possessively. It felt as if she had done it a thousand times before. It felt spine-tinglingly new. She gave a sigh of perfect content.

'Happy?' she asked, although she knew the answer.

Gil stretched lazily, though he did not remove the hand on her breast.

'I'll do.'

She turned her head. 'You'll do?' she echoed in mock outrage. 'You'll *do*?' She hauled herself up on her elbow to look down at him. 'You have the most mind-blowing experience of the decade and all you can say is you'll do?'

He traced her mouth idly. In the flickering light she could see that his eyes were dancing.

'Seems to cover it.'

She collapsed on his chest, laughing softly. 'I suppose it does.'

He gathered her close again, pulling the covers up over her bare shoulders. The protectiveness of the gesture moved her to the heart. Possessive in her turn, she kissed the bare, warm shoulder.

'How do you feel?'

He groaned.

'No, I mean it. How do you feel?'

His arm tightened round her. 'Right.'

'What?'

She reared up to look at him. Gil smiled right into her eyes.

'Right,' he repeated softly. 'Like everything fits and the problem is solved. Just—right.'

'Oh,' said Bella on a long, wondering note.

She wanted to tell him that she felt the same. That she had never, ever, felt so complete. Or so completely happy.

But the day was taking its toll. Her eyelids drooped. Once, twice, she jerked herself awake, wanting to tell him she loved him. But sleep was too strong for her.

Her head came to rest in the crook of his shoulder. His arm curved round her. Her breathing lengthened, relaxed, quietened.

Gil held her against the steady rise and fall of his chest. He felt her limbs slacken, her head grow heavy. She slept, while he watched the shadows.

He was frowning. He had seen something in her tonight that he would never have imagined. His passionate tango dancer had a secret that made her flinch just to think of it. He wanted to draw the splinter, to make her realise that whatever had happened in the past was over. That the future was the two of them. And it was going to be glorious.

No past mistake was ever going to matter to her again. No matter how much she might think it hurt now. Their shared future was going to wipe it out. He would see to it.

I will keep her safe, he promised himself. *I will keep her safe.*

In the morning, everything was different.

Coming awake in a strange bed, at first Bella did not know where she was. She knew she was cold, though. There should have been arms round her. She was sure that she was not supposed to be alone this morning, though she was a bit hazy on the details.

Then a laughing voice out of memory said, *'We exchanged pheromones!'*

Bella sat bolt upright. No, of course she was not supposed to be alone. Where was Gil? He hadn't had second thoughts, had he?

No, she thought, wrapping her arms round herself. No, he wouldn't have had second thoughts. Not after last night.

Another remark curled like mist out of that night in New York. *'I only do one thing at a time.' Boy, oh, boy, he certainly does*, thought Bella, purring at last night's memories. She found she was smiling with her whole body.

Still, he should be here to remind her in person. She gave up trying to sleep and went to look for him.

She found him outside among a scene of devastation. The village green was littered with fallen branches, roof tiles and various detritus that the wind had picked up and dumped. The road was blocked by a fallen tree. There were five or six people there, wandering round in silence. They looked stunned.

Except for Gil. He was, she saw, quietly taking charge. Bella was beginning to wonder if he had it in him to feel normal stuff at all.

How could he have left their bed without a word to come and organise a civic removal operation? And he was doing it so well too. No raised voices. No arguments. Just a steady eye on the goal and total persistence. Every time anyone dropped one of the saws or ropes and looked round in dismay, Gil was there. He encouraged them. Sometimes he made them laugh. But he was absolutely determined to get them back on track, pulling with the communal effort. And he did.

'One thing at a time', thought Bella, chilled. *This time it's not me. So he's put me out of his mind.* She realised that the tabby-cat sweater was no protection at all against the cold.

He saw her. She knew he saw her because he raised a hand and smiled. But it was not the right smile. It was friendly enough, as friendly as he was to everyone else who was doing what he told them to do, but it was not intimate. It certainly did not say, You're special, nor, This lady is mine. It said—

'Hi.' He did not even come over to her. He certainly did not kiss her. All that passion last night and he did not even *kiss* her. 'You're up. Good. We can do with another pair of hands.'

Bella felt herself ice up. It was a feeling she recognised.

She said quietly, 'I'll get a coat.'

CHAPTER EIGHT

BELLA worked hard, hauling lopped branches. It broke all the nails that had been so smartly shaped and painted for the wedding. She hardly noticed. She did not notice the biting cold or the wobbly front wheel on the wheelbarrow either. She was too busy watching Gil. And realising that, in spite of the revelatory intimacies of last night, she really did not know him at all.

When the road was clear at last and the dead tree was disappearing down the road behind a local tractor, she sat down for the first time. Her legs were shaking.

Gil strode up, carrying the last of the mighty branches. He was laughing. His hair was all over the place and his shirt was torn. It revealed a surprisingly muscular shoulder. Except, of course, it was no surprise to Bella who had slept with her mouth against those muscles.

But that was last night, she thought desolately. *This is morning. And a big hello to common sense!*

Gil dropped his burden. 'You're looking gloomy. What's wrong?'

Gloomy! Bella glared at him. Well, she was not to let him see how rejected she felt. And she was not going to let herself even think that rejection mattered.

So she said the first thing that came into her head. 'I've broken my nails.'

He blinked. 'Is that a problem?'

'I work at a fashion magazine,' said Bella improvising wildly. 'It's not going to look good. I shall have to get a manicure before I can go into work.'

He grinned down at her. He had dirt on his cheek and the brown eyes were brilliant. He looked wickedly sexy.

'Then, don't go.'

Bella looked at up. For a moment she almost thought he was asking her to stay with him. But then she saw the laughing challenge. No, he wasn't asking her to stay. Oh, he wanted her. But he wanted her *available*. Not with him. Not close and committed for ever.

Well, she couldn't blame him. Why on earth should he want her for ever? They did not have that sort of relationship. They had fireworks and passion and nothing to say to each other in the morning, while he went off and ran the world. He had never said anything to suggest otherwise. It was stupid to hope for it. They were poles apart. He was nearly a professor and she was a party girl.

She said quietly, 'I don't think that would be a sensible idea, do you?'

The gleam died out of his eyes. 'No, I suppose not.'

All of sudden he looked tired.

Bella could only pick at the breakfast the small hotel provided. Gil ate a hearty meal. All through it, people wandered up, talking about the road clearing operation, other disasters further up the route to London, life. Clearly they had taken him to their hearts.

'They'll be giving you the freedom of Toytown next,' said Bella.

It was meant to be joke but it sounded waspish, the way it came out. Gil looked at her narrowly.

'What's wrong?'

'Nothing.'

'You're not really worried about that silly job, are you?'

'It's not silly,' said Bella, firing up. 'It's my first go at a career and I love it. I'm very lucky to have this opportunity.'

'So, if I asked you to stay, the answer would be no?'

She gave a hard little laugh. 'I don't answer hypothetical questions.'

His eyes were very steady.

'OK. Forget the hypothesis. Stay with me.'

But she was too wretched to listen. Or maybe too scared.

She had never felt like this. She had thought she had broken her heart last year when Kosta had looked at her kindly and had shut the door in her face. Now she was beginning to think that she had not even scratched the surface of heartbreak. And she had not seen it coming this time.

She was desperate to be alone and regroup her forces. Or she would fall apart.

So she said, 'I've got to be back at work tomorrow morning. I promised.' And went on saying it.

In the end, Gil did as she asked and took her straight to the airport.

On the concourse, he turned her to face him.

'Bella, what is it?' he said urgently. 'What happened?'

The crowd jostled them. She staggered as her foot slipped on the industrial shiny floor. He grabbed her hands and held on to them but she still felt a thousand miles away. It was the place, she thought, like a hospital, so bright and impersonal, with all these little personal dramas all around them that did not amount to a row of beans.

'Bella.' He shook her gently. He sounded exasperated but so far away. Even his voice was different, spiralling up to high girders over their heads and getting lost.

She detached her hands gently.

'Nothing happened.'

'Bella!'

'Thank you for driving me here.'

'So that's it, is it?'

Suddenly his eyes were dangerous. It shook Bella out of her fatalistic cocoon, at least for a moment.

'What?'

'A little dalliance after the festivities, then thank you and goodbye!'

She blinked. What was wrong with him? That was what he wanted, wasn't it? She nearly said so.

But Gil didn't give her time. He was saying. 'I don't know why I'm surprised. I even heard you, didn't I, saying you weren't ready to commit?' The sudden attack was savage. 'Annis and Kosta can do it. But you don't fancy it.'

Maybe if he hadn't mentioned Kosta... Maybe if he hadn't mentioned Annis, whom her mother thought he might be in love with...

Maybe if he hadn't looked through her this morning…

Bella felt as if she had been drenched in ice.

She said furiously, 'You want to know what happened? All right, I'll tell you.'

She tore her hands away and stepped back.

'I was in love with Kosta,' she said in a thin, precise voice. Her throat hurt. 'I thought he— Well, it doesn't matter. He barely knew Annis then. It never occurred to me— Well, that doesn't matter either. At the time, I thought he was writing me off as too young and silly. So I thought, I'll show him I'm a modern woman. There's no point in hanging around. If you want something, go for it.'

She gave a shrug with a self-mocking laugh. That hurt too.

Gil was staring at her. His face had gone impassive again. Only his eyes burned.

'So I gave it my best shot. I turned up at his door at midnight. Bottle of champagne. No bus fare home. No underwear.'

He made a strangled sound.

'It's all right. He didn't know. We never got far enough for him to find out.' She swallowed and gave him a glittering, painful smile. 'He called a cab and paid him to take me home. Very smooth.'

Gil looked as if he had been carved in stone. 'You're saying that last night was about running away from Kosta Vitale?'

Bella shrugged again. She looked away.

'I don't believe you.'

She glanced up at the departures board. Her flight was blinking. She picked up her overnight bag and looped it over her shoulder.

'Sorry about that.' She could not have sounded less sorry if she'd tried.

'I don't believe it,' he said again more strongly.

She turned back to him and met his eyes.

'But, then, you were telling me—you're no good at reading women, are you?' she said cruelly.

Gil froze.

Bella walked away.

She slept on the plane. She would have said it was dreamless. But when she woke up there were tears on her face.

The next month was a nightmare. She threw herself into work but it was no distraction. At the back of her mind all the time was Gil's face. She did not think she would ever forget it.

He had gone so absolutely still. Why on earth had she told him? She had never told anyone about that horrible night at Kosta's flat! She had hardly admitted it to herself. Gil must have been *disgusted.*

Every time she thought about it, Bella winced physically. Once she'd actually jumped in her seat at work. She had been trying to concentrate on proofreading her article and the memory had just crept up on her. Shocked, she'd clapped her hands to suddenly burning cheeks and had said out loud, 'Oh, *no*!'

'Is that a woman with a nasty secret, I hear?' said Sally, passing on her way to the photocopier.

'Secret?' Bella's laugh was a groan. 'Haven't got a single secret left.'

'Sounds bad.'

'It is. I splurged them all on the last man—' She broke off. 'Never mind.'

Sally looked at her shrewdly. 'We're not talking the guy from finance, right?'

Bella was bewildered. 'Which guy?'

'Thought not,' said Sally with satisfaction. 'I mean, you weren't really interested, I know. But you didn't actually look *through* the poor guy. Not until you went home to your sister's wedding. What happened?'

'Nothing,' said Bella, so ferociously that even Sally blinked. She was not talking to Sally though. She was talking to herself.

* * *

To begin with Gil rang several times. Every time she got home there were messages on her machine. His tone varied from sweet reason to icy exasperation but the message was basically always all the same.

'Call me.'

Only the numbers he told her to call changed. He was obviously travelling all round the world. She wrote them down. But she never called any of them.

In the end the messages ceased. Bella told herself it was a relief. That did not stop her calling up her home phone every hour to check whether a new message had come in. But Gil had gone off the air.

Eventually she found out why, thanks to Annis.

Back from her honeymoon, it seemed that Annis had nothing better to do than keep Bella informed on the progress of her business consultancy. So one May morning, Bella went to her computer and found she had an email waiting for her on *Elegance Magazine*'s central register. It was headed 'My First Millionaire!'

Under this dramatic heading, Annis's voice was as familiar as if she was in the room, not on the other side of the Atlantic.

Hi!
Thought you'd like to see this. I'm cock-a-hoop about it. Kosta keeps saying I shouldn't get excited, it's bad for the baby. But I think the baby ought to share his mother's triumphs. Heaven knows, there will be plenty of disasters for him to get used to. I've dropped the baby doll three times at the parental practice night. And at the antenatal class, I kicked the woman in front of me halfway across the room. She and her partner slid like the British bobsleigh team. Not sure I'm cut out for this motherhood thing. Kosta says to stop worrying. By the time our child can compare notes with proper parents, he'll be past caring. But I'm going to make sure that he knows I'm a very good management consultant. *He's got to have some respect.*

Bella grinned. That sounded like Annis. But the next sentence made her grin die abruptly.

So forget Bugs Bunny. The son and heir is getting Gil de la Court pasted on his bedroom wall.
Love, Annie.
PS Love the photo. He's so brainy, you forget the man's gorgeous with it.

Heart sinking, Bella opened the attachment.

It was quite a short article. It seemed to be from a newspaper in Sydney.

Gilbert de la Court is the newest member of the exclusive club of Net Millionaires. He launched Watifdotcom last month. This has seen off practised sharks who were snapping round de la Court's small company of old college friends, looking to strip out the ground-breaking randomised filter programme. It has also made de la Court and his mates millionaires overnight.

'We're just getting used to it,' says de la Court, a quiet-spoken dynamo. 'We wanted to keep our research capacity independent and we've managed that. The millionaire stuff is an unexpected bonus. We're just computer nerds who love pushing the boundaries.'

Industry watchers say this modesty is typical but deceptive. De la Court left his university teaching post to set up the company only three years ago and has seen it go from strength to strength. Since he brought in new-kid-on-the-block consultancy guru Annis Carew, the market has been waiting for him to make his move. This is expected to be only the first of many. Welcome to a new Net Star.

And the picture was, as Annis had said, gorgeous. Horribly, memorably gorgeous.

For some reason the paper had pictured him at the helm of a yacht. It looked like a holiday photograph. He was wearing ragged shorts and his hair was too long again. The digital picture on her screen showed in cruel detail how the muscles bunched in his tanned shoulders as he swung the wheel. The dark eyes were narrowed against the sun. He looked alert, intent and vividly alive.

Bella felt her heart turn over in sheer longing.

'Nice,' said Sally approvingly, leaning over her shoulder.

Bella jumped. 'Do you think so?'

'Who is he?'

'Oh, just a client of my sister's.'

'Lucky sister.'

Bella shook her head. 'My sister doesn't care,' she said in a constrained tone. 'She just got married to the love of her life.'

Sally leaned forward to get a closer look. 'If I were you, I'd ask her to pass along his phone number.'

'I've already got his phone number,' said Bella, goaded.

Sally grinned, unrepentant. 'In that case, lucky you.'

Bella threw a paper-clip at her.

Sally caught it, laughing. 'You'd better be nice to me. Or I'll tell Gary in finance about his rival.'

But it was not Gary she told. It was Rita Caruso. In front of the whole department.

It was an editorial meeting about the July edition.

'OK,' said Caruso, about two thirds into the meeting. 'Millionaires of the Month. We're going to have to do better. April was the pits.'

The journalist responsible bridled but everyone else reluctantly agreed.

'He was eighty and lived in a condo in Florida,' said the beleaguered journalist in defence of her piece. 'Find me an undiscovered millionaire who doesn't.'

'Well,' said Caruso, looking like a cat that had got the cream. 'Someone may just have done that. Bella? Do you want to tell us about "My First Millionaire"?'

Bella was sketching masks of tragedy on her note pad. And then giving them yachtsman's shoulders. And scrubbing them out. Hearing her name, she jumped.

'What?'

'The email in your inbox this morning. Who's the guy?'

Too late, Bella remembered that incoming mail went straight to central collection area, in order that any crank mail could be filtered out. Anyone could search that index. Caruso, they all knew, regularly did a search and find on key words. Millionaire, Bella now realised, had to be one of them.

Why on earth couldn't Annis have found a better title for her message, thought Bella, irritated.

She said, 'It was only a message from my sister.'

'And?'

'About a mutual—er—friend.'

'So you know this millionaire?' said Caruso tapping her rolled-gold pen against her teeth. 'What's he like?'

That was when Sally intervened.

'A hunk,' she said helpfully. 'And Bella has his phone number.'

'Great.' Caruso's eyes gleamed. 'OK. Let's have his details.'

'But I don't know any details,' said Bella alarmed.

'Then do the research. You're a journalist, aren't you?' Caruso prepared to move onto the next subject. 'Let me have what you find by the end of the day.'

So Bella reluctantly went to work. She found his academic site and printed off a couple of archived papers on Internet development which Gil had written and posted there. A general search also revealed more recent newspaper clippings. The clippings varied from enthusiastic to adulatory. She managed to lose the more breathless ones, along with all the photographs. Though she did print off a dramatically brooding one from an Internet magazine and slipped it into her shoulder bag.

She took the folder into Caruso with bad grace.

'De la Court,' said the features editor, leaning through the sheaf of press clippings at the advertising manager. 'Some guy was talking about him at dinner last night. He's the new cyber millionaire. There's got to be a story in this.'

Bella managed to look bored. She was really pleased with the result.

'He's just another geek in an anorak.'

'Geek!' Caruso gave a high-pitched crow of laughter. 'I just love it when you're superior. So British.'

Bella scowled. She knew when she was being sent up. 'Geeks aren't sexy.'

Caruso stopped laughing. 'You're missing the point here,' she said. 'He's an unmarried geek with a sudden infusion of personal wealth. This is more than sexy. It is the fairy tale.'

Bella snorted.

Caruso's eyes were steely behind her designer spectacles. 'Don't knock anything that gives our readers hope.'

Bella muttered under her breath. Caruso ignored her.

'Now, what I want you to do is this. Call him. Tell him what you've dug out.' She waved a hand at the clippings. 'Be as controversial as you like. Challenge him. Do one of your hatchet jobs if you want. *But get him to comment.* Understand?'

Oh, yes, Bella understood. Her stomach was already in free fall at the prospect. But after six months in the job she was much too experienced to say so. Caruso was not given to indulging in compassion. If she thought that Bella had any history with her chosen Millionaire of the Month, her only concern would be how to use it to spice up the article.

'Yes,' said Bella with minimal expression.

'Good. Amazing as it sounds, I have great hopes of you.' She tipped back her leather chair and looked up at Bella with a winning smile. 'To be honest, I wasn't keen when they wanted you to join us here. I don't like amateurs. I don't like trainees. And I *really* don't like daddy's little rich girls. But you're all right.'

'Thank you,' said Bella, warmed in spite of herself.

'You've got the instinct. You knew you had no experience but you made that work for you. Your New in Town pieces were cool. You work hard. You party, but you make that work for you too. You've got your finger on a pulse. Hi, to my correspondent from the metropolitan young.'

'All in all, quite an asset, then,' said Bella coolly. 'So why waste it on a piece like the Millionaire of the Month? Anyone could do that.'

Caruso stopped smiling. 'Don't push your luck. Do you want a permanent job or not? It's next month you leave us, isn't it?'

Suddenly Bella was alert. 'A job? Here?'

'Probably in London but you'd still do stuff for us. London's hot. We can use someone like you.' Caruso examined her nails. 'You'd have to take the assignments you were given, of course.'

'You mean I've got to do this millionaire piece or I've lost my chance of a job,' interpreted Bella.

'You have to do it *well*, or you've lost the chance of a job,' corrected Caruso amiably. 'That's market forces for you.'

Bella set her jaw. 'OK. But I still thinks it's dull.'

Caruso yawned. 'Up to you to make it sound *not* dull.'

Bella knew she was beaten. She picked up the file and went to the door.

'Oh, Bella…'

Caruso was pulling some proofs towards her across the desk but she stopped for a moment with a friendly smile. Well, as friendly as a piranha got, thought Bella.

She stopped. 'Yes?'

'Don't even try to lose that picture.'

'What do you mean? What picture?'

'I opened the attachment too. He's got a lot of muscles for a geek. I want that photograph in the magazine. Unless you can come up with something sexier.'

Bella did not even attempt to answer.

She did not telephone Gil. She did not even email him, although she had the address on the paper that had come with the fiery flowers he'd sent her on Valentine's Day. She should have thrown the paper away but for some reason she had not. Still, she was not going to admit that she knew how to get hold of him.

Instead she called Annis and explained Rita Caruso's idea for an in-depth profile. She made it sound as tacky as she could. No one, she thought, would advise their client to give an interview to a journalist who came up with an outline brief like that. Certainly not Annis, who valued dignity almost as much as privacy.

But Annis did not do her duty.

'Fine. I'll talk to him,' she said, infuriatingly obliging.

Bella could have danced with frustration.

But that was nothing to what she felt when she got into work the next day and found a message from the office of the chief executive of Watifdotcom.

'Mr de la Court will be in New York next week. He will call at *Elegance Magazine*'s premises on Tuesday or Wednesday, depending on his itinerary.'

Bella took it to Rita Caruso.

'We can't let him do this. He's jerking our chain.'

Caruso sucked her teeth, interested. 'He's jerking *your* chain,' she corrected thoughtfully. 'Cute.'

'You mean, you're just going to sit here and let him get away with it?'

Caruso inspected the ceiling. 'Just make sure you keep your cellphone with you at all times. Don't so much as go to the rest room without it. And don't turn it off ever. Not until the guy has told you what he eats for breakfast.' She diverted her gaze from the ceiling to Bella's furious face and raised an eyebrow. 'Unless you already know?'

Bella did not trust herself to speak.

'Fine,' said Caruso sweetly. 'Close the door on your way out.'

She was not, Bella promised herself, going to let Gil's imminent arrival have any effect on her private life. She was *not* going to sit at home and wait for him to call. Still less to turn up on the doorstep. She was going to go out and have *fun*. And then somehow, anyhow, she would get through Tuesday with her sanity intact. Unless he arrived on Wednesday, of course.

At some point in the small hours of Sunday morning, she found herself in Hombre y Mujer. She was not looking for Gil. Of course she wasn't. But when the only faces she recognised were New York residents, she flung herself into a series of wild routines that even attracted the attention of a world weary dancers' agent. She accepted his card without interest and turned away, rapping on the bar and pointing to a bottle of mineral water.

The barman was impressed. 'Hey, Paco,' he called to his boss. 'We got a star being discovered here.'

Paco lounged over. He raised his eyebrows when he saw Bella.

'Well, well, well. Welcome back. Bella, isn't it? And present obsession of my old friend Gil de la Court.'

It was too dark under the strobes for him to see how hard she flushed, Bella assured herself.

'I'm flattered,' she said, not meaning it. 'But obsession is surely going a bit far.'

He shrugged. 'Well, you know Gil.'

'N-not really.'

'He calls all the time to ask if you've been in. And who you're with.'

'*Oh!*' Bella recovered quickly but she was shaken. 'Bet it's not the first time he's asked about a woman.

Paco looked at her oddly. 'First time I've seen it.'

In fact Paco had been mildly surprised at Gil's reaction to the blonde dancer. Of course everything Gil did, he did a hundred per cent. But this pursuit was unprecedented. In his experience it was usually women who did the pursuing, while Gil responded with beautifully mannered bewilderment.

'Gil on the hunt is a new phenomenon,' he said wryly. 'I'd have said he's the last man in the world to pick up strange blondes in nightclubs. He takes his relationships seriously.'

He sounded surprisingly disapproving. He was a nightclub owner, after all, not normally a profession that doubled as arbiter of morality, thought Bella, with fury.

'Well, excuse me for breathing,' she said evilly. 'Is it my fault he's decided he wants to give himself a fling now he's a millionaire?'

She was remembering a little too clearly what he had said at the wedding. *'All that fire. All that passion… What do I have to do to get her back, my Tina?'*

That was what it was all about, she realised suddenly. That was *it*!

Gil was a man who had always taken his relationships seriously. Suddenly there was this party girl who could dance him off his feet and he had found that it was possible not to be quite so serious. Hadn't he?

She had even told as much, herself! *'It's not supposed to be a tool for anything. It's supposed to be fun.'* Heaven help her she had actually *said* that to him! So it wasn't really surprising that he had walked out on her the morning after they'd made love, was it? She had licensed him to do just that, with her own stupid, shallow words.

Paco leaned towards her, one elbow on the bar.

'So what do I tell him?'

Bella did not answer at once. For a moment she felt so wild with shame and loss that she wanted to throw her water in his face and march out. But, of course, she could not do that, it would not be cool. And if she was nothing else, she was cool.

So she took a swig from the water bottle, fighting to handle these turbulent and unwelcome feelings. And made a discovery. It was not Paco she was angry with. It was not even herself. It was Gil.

She looked at Paco, eyes narrowed, jaw tight, and said just what she meant, no subterfuge, no irony, no pretending. She could handle it after all.

'Tell him?' She slammed the bottle back on the bar. 'Tell him to do his own asking.'

She turned away without another word.

Yes! thought Paco exultantly.

Salsa babe or not, she had the mettle to meet Gil on his own terms. Maybe the man knew what he was doing after all.

*   *   *

Paco said as much to Gil the next morning, with the frankness of an old friend, when Gil called yet again.

'Go for it,' he concluded. 'Do your own asking like the girl says. May the best man win.'

'He will.' Gil sounded as determined as Paco had ever heard him.

He grinned. Gil might be determined. But the blonde looked as if she had a will of her own as well. He said that too.

'I know it.'

'Good luck, then.'

'Thank you,' said Gil drily. Paco could hear the smile in his voice. 'I think I'm going to need it.'

Bella did not sleep much on Monday night. Not surprising in the circumstances. On Tuesday she hit the ceiling every time her phone rang. By the end of the day, her nerves were in tatters, her computer files in complete disarray, and her waste-paper basket full. Gil did not call.

On Tuesday night she did not sleep at all.

On Wednesday the morning light in the bathroom was pitiless. Bella glared at the cruelly illuminated wreck that was her face and thanked God for cosmetics.

Even perfect skin was not proof against no sleep at all. She put on the full make-up she would normally not have bothered with before the cocktail hour: light-as-air compressed powder that the magazine had just received some samples of; blusher the same tone as her discreet lip gloss; tiny, discreet touches of highlighter to make her blue eyes look huge and sparkling.

She watched the sunken-eyed zombie in the mirror disappear with a certain satisfaction. Six months ago she could not have managed that. But six months ago she had never been near an up-market magazine's editorial department or a fashion shoot. These days she knew the tricks of the trade. Well, some of them.

'Whey, hey, what are you hiding?' said one of the journalists from the beauty section.

Bella was standing behind a triangular table, unwinding herself from four feet of pashmina scarf when the woman stopped by.

Bella paused. 'Why should I be hiding anything?'

'Siren Dust by Ariane, two hundred and twenty dollars the pot. We did a feature on it last month. Nice to know the samples are getting a workout.'

'Oh.'

'Don't worry, no one else will notice. But skin is my thing. And even you don't have a face like silk at nine o'clock in the morning.'

She passed on.

Bella peered in her little make-up mirror. But she was right. No one else was going to see at a casual glance that Bella had spent the night sitting in the Shaker chair, beating herself up over the past she couldn't change and a man she couldn't have. But anyone who looked closely would see it.

Would Gil look closely?

Would Gil even be here today?

She stuffed the mirror back in her bag so hard she broke a nail. Then she settled herself at the computer and logged on. The machine burped politely and told her that she had twenty two emails in her postbox. Not one of them was from Gil. Or even from the anonymous lady who ran the office of the chief executive of Watifdotcom.

Bella sighed and took a life-giving swig of coffee.

'What's up?' said Sally. 'Nerves about the millionaire?'

Bella flung the mouse away from her. 'That Siren Dust is a rip-off,' she announced.

'What?'

'Over two hundred dollars a throw and people keep asking me what's wrong. I must look like death.

Sally grinned. 'You look like a Botticelli angel, English, just like you always do. He'll think it's his birthday. But if you're drinking office coffee there must be something really wrong. Can't you wait for the Starbuck's run?'

'No,' said Bella with feeling.

That was when the phone rang.

'I have a Mr de la Court for Ms Carew,' said the laminated receptionist from the front desk. She was using her best, soap-opera, husky drawl. Clearly Gil was having an effect.

Bella gave a small scream, dropped the phone, picked it up, felt her heart race until she could hardly breathe…

And went to meet him.

The receptionist was standing up, leaning forward, tracing something on a map for him. Her auburn hair was wavy and scented and looked about as real as the princess out of a horror comic. She was letting it brush the severe dark jacket of his business suit. Gil, Bella saw, was not fighting her off.

She stepped forward smartly.

'Hello there.' Why on earth did she sound so vilely *breezy*? Like some mad kindergarten teacher, determined to pretend she was on top of things. Or a Stepford Wife.

She made it worse by sticking out her hand like a robot arm and shaking hands with quite unnecessary vigour.

'Nice to see you again,' she said to Gil, for the benefit of the Titian-haired temptress on the reception desk.

She had only seen him in a suit once before. Well, a city suit like this. He had worn a grey morning coat at the wedding, like all the other men, acceding to Lynda's request for formality. But the rest of the time Bella had known him he had been dressed casually, carelessly, as if he could not remember what he had put on. Now his charcoal grey with the nearly invisible pinstripe made him look like a stranger. Like a man very much in control, clever and suave and horribly grown-up. Like a man she did not know.

Like Caruso's Millionaire of the Month, thought Bella. She was surprised at the sharp stab of disappointment that came with the thought.

She detached her hand and gestured to a small alcove.

'Shall we talk?'

'It's what I'm here for,' said the suave, city sex god with amusement.

Bella fought to stay cool. 'Yes. Well. It's good of you to fit me in,' she said with a wide false smile. 'We're very enthusiastic about this interview.'

He raised an eyebrow. 'Are we?'

She swallowed. How did he manage to look so sexy when he was dressed exactly like her father dressed to go to work every morning? It wasn't *fair*!

Trying for brisk efficiency, she said, 'Or maybe you would prefer me to run through our questions on the telephone? I know you're fitting me in between meetings.'

But every word Gil said was proving her wrong. He said yes to coffee, yes to fighting his way through potted palms to sit among the obelisks in the alcove, yes to having read Bella's piece in the April edition, of which copies were scattered artistically on the top of a minor obelisk.

He even congratulated her, though he looked as if he had never read any magazines except the financial ones in his life. To crown it all, instead of draining his coffee, answering Bella's questions and going about his business, he was leaning back among the uncomfortable turquoise cushions and *making conversation.*

How can you bear to make conversation with a woman you have held in your arms and loved to the point of madness? How can you expect her to make conversation back? Bella did not know if she was more amazed or offended. It was rather alarming to find that what she really felt was hurt.

She looked blindly down at her neat list and jumped on a subject at random. 'Were you surprised when the Watifdotcom flotation attracted so much interest?'

'No. Why did you walk away from me at the airport?'

Bella set her teeth and did not answer. 'When did you start being interested in computers?'

'When I was six,' he said absently. 'Why haven't you answered any of my calls?'

'I didn't want to.' She sent him a challenging look. 'Why should I?'

He folded his lips together. Was he suppressing a smile? Damn it, what right had he to laugh at her?

'Why did you leave university teaching?' she snapped. 'Not enough money in it?'

'I still teach. Just not all the time. That's because I like inventing things. Have you been out partying? Enjoying New York?'

'New York's fabulous,' said Bella, crushingly.

He looked round. 'Fabulous indeed. You like all this glamour?' he asked curiously.

Bella followed his glance.

The premises of *Elegance Magazine* were redecorated on a rolling cycle but the entrance hall was essentially the same as the original design from 1922. Black lacquer cabinets, heavily decorated with Egyptian motifs, hid a space-station's supply of twenty-first-century electronic equipment. Under discreet daylight simulation palm trees flourished. Lotus blossoms, etched into glass doors, sparkled. Walnut panels shone. Rosewood and ebony inlay gleamed like sunshine.

It was an expensive designer concept that gave Bella visual indigestion. Suddenly she could not bear not to say so.

'It looks like the set for a silent movie,' she said flatly.

This time Gil did not pretend he wasn't laughing. She met his eyes defiantly.

'OK, I'm lucky to be here. It's a great opportunity and not one that most people have. I know all that. It doesn't mean I have to buy the whole box of tricks. This is naff and no one's going to brainwash me into saying anything different.' She prodded an obelisk disparagingly. 'Look at that.'

Gil inspected it. 'What is it?'

'There's a house telephone in there somewhere. Twelve feet of phallic symbol to hide a phone. Ghastly.'

Gil enjoyed it. 'Have you told them that?'

'Not yet. I'm saving it up for my farewell piece.' She recalled the reason they were together. Constraint returned. 'After I've done the interview with you.'

'It's so important to you, this interview?' His voice was level.

'Only my professional reputation,' said Bella. She wished it wasn't true. 'No interview and I can kiss goodbye to a job when my time is up. I'm sort of on probation, you see.'

'I see.' He frowned deeply.

Bella tried hard not to hold her breath.

He made up his mind. 'In that case you must have your interview. Of course you must. Only, not here. Not now.'

Instantly she was on the alert.

'If you're asking me out on a date, forget it.'

'You don't date?' he mused. 'Yes, Paco said something like that. But I found it difficult to believe. A raver like you.' He gave her an affable smile, just a hint of a question in the cool brown eyes.

'I date as much as I want.'

But she didn't. She didn't. She had turned down Gary in finance regularly. Only yesterday she had gone home alone after a solitary supper. And had sat up all night in her Shaker chair remembering.

And, oh boy, what she remembered! Not this business-suited man with his secret laughter and his cool, cool eyes. The other one. The one she had fallen in love with. Wild dancer, determined pursuer, disconcerting arguer, intense lover—she stopped herself abruptly.

Fallen in love with?

The thought struck her like a blow. She stared at him, arrested.

Was that why she was angry with him? Why she'd wanted him to call and yet hadn't answered the telephone when he had? Why she'd been so hurt when he'd left her to wake up alone?

She had a sudden vision of herself in that warm rumpled bed, waking into the cold morning and wanting to tell him she loved him.

Of course she was in love with him. She had been in love with him for ages. Long before she'd watched Annis look at Kosta and the knife had turned in her heart. It had not been at the loss of Kosta. It had been because Gil was not looking at her like that. Had never shown any sign of looking at her like that.

Oh, he'd enjoyed his Tina the Tango Dancer, with her vitality and her city cool. But he did not *love* her. If he loved her he would not have left her to wake up alone.

He was saying, 'And that's something else we need to talk about.'

She said mechanically, 'What is?'

'Dating, dancing and what you said to my friend Paco.'

How could she have been so stupid? What did she know about him after all? Except that off the leash he danced like a dervish and her mother thought he was in love with Annis?

Another one! She castigated herself savagely. Another clever, sophisticated, complicated man who was a natural mate for her clever, complicated half sister. Who had nothing at all in common with party girl Bella, no matter how much he might enjoy going wild on the dance floor once in while. Not just the dance floor, of course.

Tears pricked shamefully. She widened her eyes against them. What an *idiot* she was.

Almost at random she said, 'What did I say to your friend Paco, then?'

Gil looked at her very steadily for a moment. '"Tell him to do his own asking,"' he quoted softly.

'Oh.'

'So here I am. Asking.'

Bella looked at the clock on the opposite wall. It had a headdress and paws like a sphinx and she hated it. But if she stared at it long enough, the stupid tears would subside.

'My dating habits are nothing to do with you,' she retorted.

Bad temper worked every time. The tears went into retreat.

Gil gave a little nod, as if it was no more than he expected. 'You're going to be difficult,' he diagnosed.

'I am not,' said Bella between her teeth, 'being difficult.'

He gave her a forgiving smile that made her want to hit him. 'Don't worry about it. I like difficult women.'

'No one has ever called me difficult.'

'That's probably because you've ridden roughshod over them, poor souls,' said Gil blithely. 'Understandable, gorgeous girl like you. Well, you won't do that with me. You'd better get used to the idea.'

Bella blinked. There was enough truth in that to silence her though she had no idea how he had uncovered it. Unless he had been talking to Annis again?

The thought made her writhe inwardly.

She said harshly, 'What do you want?'

He smiled. '*You* want to interview me. And I want to help you achieve your ambition.'

'Oh?'

'Among other things,' he conceded. 'So I thought we could kill several birds with one stone. I'm going to my house in Greece tomorrow. Come with me.'

'*What?*'

He repeated the outlandish invitation. Except it wasn't an invitation. It was a command.

'I can't,' said Bella in pure instinct.

'Why not? You have a passport and no commitments. Not so much as a budgerigar.'

She did not ask him how he knew that. 'I have a life. My work…'

'This is work, or so I thought. Would you like me to clear it direct with your boss?'

There was no way Caruso would let her get out of it. She would probably pack her bag for her.

'No,' said Bella hastily.

'And you don't date,' he reminded her blandly. 'So there's no trouble there.'

Their eyes locked. He was laughing gently. But there was something quite implacable about the look in his eyes.

There was a little flame in their depths that made her urgently and shiveringly aware that under the conservative grey suiting there was a body that she knew as well as she knew her own.

'This is not fair,' she said under her breath.

'Then, we're quits.'

'What?' she said again, bewildered.

'Do you think it was fair to throw a bomb like that at the airport and then walk away through passport control where you knew I couldn't follow you?'

He was suddenly steely. Bella blinked.

'I don't understand,' she said, not entirely truthfully.

Gil raised his eyebrows. 'Then I'll explain,' he promised. 'But not here and not unless you meet me halfway.'

Bella hesitated, torn.

'In Greece.'

In the face of such determination, she had no defence. After all, half of her mind was on his side. Along with all her heart.

Bella gave in.

'What can I say?' She flung out her hands, with a self-mocking laugh.

Gil touched her cheek fleetingly. Possessively.

'Good decision. Pick you up at six.'

Bella felt as if the world had shot away from under her.

'Tonight?' She gasped.

'Certainly tonight. I think we've both waited long enough,' he said in a judicial tone. 'Don't you?'

He touched his fingers to her parted lips in a pantomime of a kiss.

And before she could protest—or respond—or say anything at all—he was gone.

'Tonight,' he said over his shoulder, as if he did not care who heard him.

It was a promise.

CHAPTER NINE

AS BELLA had predicted, Rita Caruso was only too delighted to wave her off to Greece. She provided her with a camera, an *Elegance Magazine* charge card and some dubious vocational advice.

'Don't forget, look for the secrets. The secrets are what makes him human.'

'Great,' muttered Bella.

She flung what clothes she could find that would do for a Greek island into an overnight bag. She did not really have any summer gear with her. It had been winter when she'd come to New York. Even now, the evenings were cool. She did not have anything to swim in. She certainly did not have any sun cream.

'How hot is it in Greece at this time of the year?' she asked Gil in the yellow cab to the airport.

'Hot enough to put some colour in your cheeks,' he told her. 'You look terrible.'

So much for Siren Dust!

'I'll sue that cosmetic company,' said Bella with energy. 'They give ravers like me a bad name.'

By the time they arrived in Athens, though, she was too tired to manage a single smart remark.

Gil saw it. He wafted her from the airport to the port of Piraeus without her having to do any more than smile wearily at the immigration official. As if by magic, a boat appeared at the quayside with her luggage already aboard.

'You got used to the millionaire life quickly,' mumbled Bella, but she was nearly asleep.

'Adaptability is my middle name.'

But she stumbled on the gangway. Gil did not hold back any longer. He scooped her off her feet and carried her below.

Bella did not remember much of the voyage. It was afternoon when the sound of the boat's engine changed. She came up on deck to see that they were pulling into a tiny cove. At first she thought it was deserted. But then she saw the stone jetty. The hillside was steep, covered with olive trees, but she thought she could make out rough steps leading up through the olive grove.

'Welcome to my island,' said Gil, coming up behind her.

He had changed. More than his clothes, Bella thought. No more suited man, he was wearing stone-coloured shorts and a loose T-shirt bearing the Greek letter pi in bold black script. This was the laughing yachtsman from Annis's picture. His hair gleamed like burnished wood in the sun and his arms were bare.

Wow! thought Bella. She swallowed hard but her heart started a treacherous pit-a-pat somewhere up in her throat.

To forget it she said the first thing that came into her head. 'You own an *island*? I was right, you did slip into the millionaire lifestyle easily.'

He laughed. 'My island, only in the sense of my home. All I own is the house up there.'

Bella squinted upwards to where he was pointing. She had to tilt her head back a long way.

'That's quite a climb.'

'You'll make it.' She could hear the smile in his voice. 'A superfit tango dancer like you.'

Her breath hissed as if she had run a splinter into herself. Oh, great! There it was again. Entertainment by Tina the Tango Dancer before he went back to his real life!

Except—would he have gone to so much trouble if she was only the entertainment? She looked up at the terrifying cliff.

'I'll give it my best shot,' she said grimly. She was not talking about the steep path alone.

But by the time they reached the top of the cliff she was beyond thinking about anything except how to take another step. Parts of the path were not so much steep as vertical. When Gil held out a hand and hauled her up the last few dusty yards, she had a stitch in her side and no breath left at all. By contrast, his breathing was as steady as if he had been on an afternoon stroll. Bella had the feeling that for two pins he would simply tip her off her feet and carry her the rest of the way.

Her pride revolted. So, though she let him help her up, she firmly detached herself from his helping hand as soon as she was on level ground again.

'Thank you,' she said, resisting the temptation to put a hand to her heaving side.

'No sweat. That's the last time you'll have to do it.'

For a wild moment she thought he was threatening to keep her prisoner in his cliff-top eyrie.

'What?'

'Winch,' he said succinctly. 'Now we're up here, I can engage it.'

He went to a small stone outhouse further along the cliff. Bella leaned against an olive tree and allowed herself to drag some reviving breaths into her labouring lungs.

Gil moved easily, as if he had total mastery over his body and the elements, even over the uneven stony ground. The afternoon sun turned the light tan of his skin to gold. She watched him avidly as he opened the doors to the outhouse and sent a crude lift apparatus creaking its way down the hillside. Totally absorbed, he was unaware of her scrutiny.

He was more than attractive, she realised. He was elemental, somehow in harmony with the stony landscape. He stood on the very edge of the cliff, steady as a rock. When he raised a muscular arm in response to a signal from the beach, he looked like a statue of one of the golden, athletic gods. Calm. Powerful. *Glorious.*

Oh, Lord, I've got it bad, she thought.

He certainly had grounds for all that magnificent confidence. As he started to wind the big winch, the thing began to run away and he steadied it, making it keep to the pace he wanted. Bella watched his shoulder muscles bunch and release, bunch and release with the effort. She thought, *No matter what happens in this wild place, I'll be safe with Gil.*

Except that she did not feel safe. Not exactly unsafe, either. Just uneasily aware that anything could happen. And not very sure how well she was likely to deal with most of it.

There was nothing she could do. She was here now. She would just have to do the best she could.

She unpropped her shoulders from the sustaining olive tree and went over to Gil.

'What can I do?'

He did not pause but he glanced down at her. Standing beside him as he turned the winch, Bella had a sudden revelation of how tall he was. She only came up to his brown shoulder. Why had she not noticed that before? Surely it must have been obvious. When they'd danced. When he'd carried her below on the boat. When they'd made love.

Hell, why had that popped into her mind? Now was not the time to be remembering making love with Gil de la Court.

She swallowed and said loudly, 'There must be something useful I can do.'

Fortunately he did not seem to pick up the unsettling direction of her thoughts. He was concentrating on practicalities as the cage creaked up towards them. Leaning over cautiously, Bella saw that it was now full of their luggage.

'We usually take deliveries into the house in a wheelbarrow. Not the most glamorous transport,' Gil said ruefully, 'but it works. It should be outside the kitchen door.'

He nodded towards the house.

For the first time Bella looked at the place properly. It was a single-storey building, with simple rough white walls and a roof of red curly tiles. At the moment its bright blue shutters were closed, making it look asleep. The biggest terracotta pots she had ever seen were ranged like guardsmen along the sea-facing wall under the windows. They were filled with huge pelargoniums, dark as arterial blood.

'More red flowers,' said Bella involuntarily. 'That's a colour you really go for, isn't it?'

At once she wished she had not. What was the point in harking back?

Gil did not pause in his winching. 'Colour of passion,' he said. 'There's not enough passion in my life.'

'So you go looking for it on the dance floor?' said Bella with a spurt of bitterness that she could not quite contain. 'When you're bored?'

He went very still. 'Is that what you think?' he said at last, slowly.

She looked away. 'It's obvious, isn't it?'

'That I wanted you the first moment I saw you?' he asked in a matter-of-fact tone.

Bella jumped. 'What?'

'Yes, I suppose it is pretty obvious. But, then, you must be used to it.'

She pressed her hands to her burning cheeks. 'How can you say that? People don't *say* things like that?' she protested, oddly alarmed.

'Why not? If it's the truth?'

'They just don't, that's all.'

Gil nodded, as if he was receiving new and useful information. 'The same people who think sex is just fun?' he asked politely.

She jumped more violently this time. So he remembered that wild night and what they had said to each other before it had got even wilder. He remembered the stupid things she had said to him. Oh, she had no one but herself to blame for this mess she was in.

'Yes,' she said in a stifled voice, not looking at him.

'What about you? How's the passion in your life?' he added, quite as if he were asking her to exchange notes on favourite pastimes.

Bella froze. She could feel him looking at her. Her skin prickled with awareness. She avoided his eyes.

Here it comes, she thought, *the first move in a game of anything can happen. And I'm not* ready.

She said hurriedly, 'I'll find that wheelbarrow.'

She escaped. For the moment.

The house, she found, presented its most spartan face to the sea. On the other side there was an impressive porticoed entrance. Tall windows under Moorish arches gave onto a vine-covered terrace. A paved garden rioted with herbs. A shady lemon grove climbed a further, slighter slope, shaded by lollipop pines. Beyond the vines and more pots of brilliant flowers, there was even a perimeter wall covered with nodding honey-coloured roses. The scent of blossom was overwhelming in the still, hot air but the deserted feeling was almost palpable. It felt like a sultan's summer palace waiting for its master.

It was oddly disquieting, that sensation of waiting. *As if I'm waiting too*, thought Bella.

Which had to be crazy. Modern women did not wait, well not like that. Not for the life-giving touch of some mythical hero. Modern women went out and found what they needed for themselves. Modern women took the initiative. And they certainly did not turn ordinary mortal men into gods.

Jet lag, Bella told herself ruthlessly. And an overactive imagination.

But she still did not want to go into the unlocked house alone. Instead, she circumnavigated it. The wheelbarrow turned out to be standing on its nose under the cover of a small porch by a less impressive door. She grabbed it and wheeled it back to him.

There was a surprising amount of baggage. Bella said so.

'Supplies,' said Gil briefly. 'I haven't been here this year. I missed Easter because of the stock-market launch. There'll be repairs to do. And we need provisions of course.'

Bella was surprised. 'You do the repairs yourself?'

He pushed the barrow back to the kitchen door.

'Aren't millionaires allowed to play with power tools?' asked Gil, amused. '*Elegance Magazine* rules, right?'

'No, it's not that.' She struggled to explain. 'I thought you'd have better stuff to do. I mean, you're supposed to be a genius.'

'I still need to eat and I prefer to sleep with a roof over my head,' said Gil with something of a snap. 'Survival is the same for everyone, genius or no genius.'

He began to unload the bags with economical efficiency and a faint air of annoyance.

Bella gave up and followed him into the house at last.

He went round rapidly, opening windows, unbarring shutters, letting in the scents of the sea and the hot herbal garden. Then he came back to the kitchen and began to rummage through a box of tools.

Watching, Bella made a discovery. It should have dawned on her before.

'This house isn't a millionaire's perk, is it? You've owned it for ages.'

He emerged with a spanner. 'Inherited it. My grandfather built it.'

'Your grandfather?' She did not believe it. 'That's de la Court of Sparta, I take it?'

He grinned. 'No. That's a highly romantic young scholar who came here and fell in love with the local philosopher's daughter and wouldn't go away until her family agreed to let them marry.' He looked at her over the top of the spanner, a wicked glint in his eye. 'We tend to be rather excessive in the matter of love in my family.'

Bella swallowed. Loudly. His grin widened.

But he did not touch her. Instead he disappeared into a tall cupboard. There were sounds of mechanical wrenching, a sharp swear word, and then an exclamation of triumph.

'There. Power on.'

He backed out, pushing a hand through his hair. A dusty skein of destroyed cobwebs clung to the crown. Without thinking, Bella leaned forward and pulled the grey lint off.

Gil stopped dead.

For a moment their eyes locked.

She thought, *Is this his second move in the game? Or is it my turn?*

He reached up and took her hand very carefully. It seemed as if she could not move. Could not speak. She even held her breath, though she could not have said exactly why.

He said gently, 'Bella, I'm sorry, but I'm not one of your men who think sex is just for fun. I can't behave as if I am.'

She could not think of anything to say. He gave her hand back. Then he stepped away, put the spanner back in its box and carried on talking as if nothing had happened.

But he was breathing as if he had just run up that killer cliff.

Maybe it *was* the second move, then. But she was not sure whether whatever happened next would be his choice or hers. Or in response to some inevitable pattern that neither of them could do anything about.

It was exciting. It was terrifying. It was nothing the modern woman had any training for at all.

And she did not have the slightest idea what to do next.

So she did nothing. Or rather she did what any well-behaved guest would do on any respectable social visit. She followed him round the house, taking note of bedrooms, bathrooms, light switches, bookcases…exclaiming at the view and admiring the art. Not touching him, of course. And not asking any question that might have an answer she could not deal with.

So when he said, 'Maybe you'd like to rest in your room after the journey?' She fell upon it like a reprieve.

Her room looked out onto the lemon grove. The afternoon shadows were long over a mosaic-tiled floor and a low, wide bed. Gil stood in the doorway and did not come in.

'You have your own shower room but if you want a bath, you know where it is. You remember how to work the Jacuzzi?'

He sounded like a cordial, rather bored host. It was entirely Bella's fault that her imagination immediately clamoured with pictures of the two of them in the massive tub, amid the bubbles.

'Yes,' she said, fighting her imagination for all she was worth.

'If there's anything else you want, call me. I'll be in the garden.'

'All right.'

'Unless I'm swimming. I usually swim before supper. The sea is wonderful. You could even join me.'

Bella shook her head. 'No swimsuit,' she said, not without relief.

Gil was politely unimpressed. 'I think you'll find that *Elegance Magazine* have provided one. If not, several.'

He nodded towards a suitcase that was twice the size of her own modest bag. Bella registered it for the first time.

'That's mine?'

He shrugged. 'That's what they gave me to bring.'

She knew who to thank for that. *Sally!* thought Bella.

Aloud she said, 'I'll look later. Now I'm very tired. So if you don't mind…' She gave a huge and not entirely phoney yawn.

'Of course,' said Gil, utterly courteous, utterly indifferent. Well, maybe. He still hadn't quite got his breathing under control, Bella thought with a tiny stab of triumph. 'Rest well,' he said, and left her.

She tried. She really tried.

When she woke from her uneasy doze it was dark and there was music. She showered quickly and climbed into jeans and a cotton shirt. Her *own* jeans and shirt. She did not think she was strong enough to see what seduction gear Sally had packed yet. She went in the direction of the music.

It was on the terrace. The sun had set but it was not yet quite dark. Gil was sitting under the vines, a glass of wine in his hand, his feet on the marble table, head back, listening to the unearthly sweetness that poured from speakers high up under the vines.

'What is that?' said Bella, constraint temporarily dispelled by the sheer beauty of the music.

Gil put down his wine carefully and stood up.

'An American counter-tenor. Wonderful, isn't he?' He pulled out to reach for a glass for her. 'This is his new recording.'

'I don't know much about classical music,' said Bella, constraint returning in spades. Annis loved it. Why had Bella ever thought that she and Gil could have anything in common?

But he surprised her.

'Lucky you.'

'What?'

'You've got so much delight to come.'

He poured wine from an unlabelled bottle. 'Hope you like this. It's retsina. Made by one of my relatives. I don't think anything actually died in it.'

Bella gave a little choke of laughter and sipped. The wine was cool on the palate, warm on the throat. It smelled of oregano and thyme and every Mediterranean holiday she had ever had. She said so.

'You must have an excellent palate. To me it just tastes like Jorgo's usual brew.'

The terrace chair was made of bamboo, light but comfortable. Bella relaxed into its plump cushions.

'Who's Jorgo?'

'He's married to the daughter of the son of my great uncle,' said Gil fluently, as if he had said it many times before.

Bella blinked.

He laughed. 'Degrees of relationship are very important here. There was a time when my grandfather was only allowed to own the house because of my grandmother. She was born in the mill just over the hill.'

He nodded towards the dark landscape behind them.

'Did you know her?'

He shook his head. 'She died when my father was born.' He paused, then added, 'Ours was a house without women. My own mother was killed in a road accident when I was three. There were nannies, of course, but they did what my father and grandfather told them to. So it was a very masculine upbringing. Maybe that's why I don't read women very well.'

He sounded thoughtful and a bit bewildered.

She remembered something Paco had said. *Gil on the hunt is a new phenomenon.*

She said quietly, 'Will you tell me something?'

'Anything.' It sounded very serious.

She said with difficulty, 'The woman you didn't read so well. How important was she?'

There was a small silence. Then he said, 'Shrewd of you to realise it was one particular woman.'

Of course, she should have asked, Was it Annis? She nearly did. But in the end she could not bring herself to say it aloud.

'Well?'

He shifted in his chair. He looked uncomfortable, impatient.

'More important than I wanted to admit.' He swirled the golden wine round and round, frowning over the glass. He added abruptly, 'If I'm honest, she tied me up in knots. She had all these ideas that I was supposed to know without her telling me. And they changed. I couldn't keep up.'

That didn't sound like Annis.

'In the end I gave up, of course.' A muscle moved convulsively in his cheek. 'Not soon enough, though. It's not my temperament, giving up. So I went on banging my head against a brick wall until she told me she was in love with someone else. Someone who understood her.'

But that could be Annis. And from the pain in his voice, it did not sound like an old hurt. She wished she had the courage to ask. It would make it all so simple…

'I see,' Bella said in a small voice, not asking.

He looked up quickly. 'Does that make us quits?'

She was bewildered. 'I'm sorry?'

'You told me you were afraid of your father,' he reminded her softly. 'You said you'd never told anyone before. Well, that's my contribution to the pot of secrets. I've never told anyone either.'

Bella's heart twisted. She said in stifled voice, 'I'm sorry.'

He said nothing. The angel voice sang languidly, meltingly. Beyond the terrace, the cicadas trilled. Below them, the sea curled murmurously round the headland and whispered up the beach. The stars shimmered in velvet darkness. Clouds, insubstantial as moon-breath, scudded across them, making them tremble.

Bella trembled too, not from the cool evening breeze.

At last he said in an odd voice, 'I think you are. Sorry, I mean. Oh, well.'

Bella found her eyes were full of tears. She had no idea why.

Eventually he said, 'I usually barbecue something I've caught. Didn't have time to fish today, though, so it's vegetarian tonight. OK?'

'Fine,' said Bella, wondering how she would ever force anything down her tight throat.

'And then we'll talk about how you want to run this assignment of yours.'

He got up. 'Enjoy your wine. And the music.' He tossed a CD case onto the table. 'I'll bring it out when it's ready.'

He left her staring out into the dark, more torn than she had ever been in her life. The music tumbled round her like a magic waterfall.

Ask him! said her old, brave self. *What have you got to lose?*

Hope, said the new, vulnerable Bella.

She was still batting the arguments back and forth in her head when he came back with candles and a pile of crockery.

'What can I do?'

'Light the candles.' He tossed her a box of matches and went.

The candle flames streamed a little in the breeze off the sea. Bella shivered. It was a perfect night. She had never felt this alive in her life.

Gil returned with a big dish of salad and barbecued haloumi cheese. He set it down on the marble table, and offered her a plate and a fork.

'Dig in.'

She fully expected that he would revert to his practised, civilised conversation. But he didn't.

'So tell me about this thing with Kosta,' he said when the food was finished and they sat in the light of candles and the distant stars. 'Were you serious? Did you really turn up on his doorstep with seduction in mind?'

'Certainly,' said Bella. Her flippant tone was very good, she congratulated herself.

'No underwear at all?'

'Not a stitch.'

Gil shook his head, the movement of amazement eloquent. 'Lucky chap.'

'He didn't see it quite like that.' Bella was dry. 'Put yourself in his shoes.'

'I wish!' said Gil, even drier.

Bella might have been trembling, with every sense piercingly alert, but she could still fight her corner.

'But you said you're not the sort of person who thinks sex is just for fun,' she pointed out acerbically. 'Why would you appreciate it any more than Kosta did?'

He drew a sharp breath. 'Why do you think?'

She glared, half bewildered, desirous. But he did not touch her.

It set the pattern for the days to follow.

* * *

During the day, Gil fished or swam or worked on the land out of Bella's sight. In the evening he gave her a drink and discussed what he called her assignment, encouraging her to take notes and photographs. Then he left her to listen to music and watch the haunting, beautiful darkness alone while he cooked her a meal. She struggled to eat it.

All the time he talked, about his work, his remote father, the friends he surrounded himself with, about books and music and pastimes. He was a rock climber, she found. He had never listened to Latin music before he'd met Paco and did not know one of the artists that Bella listened to every day. He hardly ever went to the movies. Never watched videos.

In return, and cautiously, Bella told him a little about her passion for children's films but she felt out of her depth all the time. He seemed to want to know about her. And yet the one thing that she knew they had in common, he never approached.

Every night they said goodnight and went to their separate beds.

Bella did not know how she could bear it. But she had no choice. Along with the suitcase of designer gear, Sally had booked her a closed-ended ticket, with a return date at the end of a week. If she left early she would have to pay her own fare, but that was not what worried her. If she returned early she would have to *explain*. And that was something she really could not bear.

So she stayed. And walked in the garden when he was on the beach. And made notes for her article. And took a rapid course in classical music from the CDs on his shelves.

There was one song in particular, a serenade that swelled and rocked like the sunlit sea below, sweet and steady and not quite sad. Bella found her body moving to its timeless sway involuntarily. She was ravished by the delicacy of the singer's voice. She had never heard anything like it. It was a physical sensation, like a gentle finger down the spine. Like love, she thought, half ashamed of the fancy.

She could not decipher the words, though. She thought they were French. She contemplated asking Gil what they meant but somehow that seemed too dangerously intimate. So she didn't.

But she did not want to stay in the house, with her emotions ripped ragged by his music. So she found the most workmanlike of Sally's exotic bikinis and put it on. She pulled a shirt of her own over it, and went down to the beach.

Gil was there, as she had half known he would be. Or rather he was in the sea. A plastic container and his fishing tackle, stacked neatly in the lee of the jetty, showed that he had caught their supper. And now he was enjoying himself.

Bella stood still and shaded her eyes. The white sand was soft and warm under her feet. She wriggled her toes luxuriously. Gil was a long way out, a black dot heading for the horizon with powerful strokes that cut through the water.

She did not know if she was disappointed or relieved. Relieved on the whole, she thought. At least he was not there to see when she dropped her nice familiar shirt and launched herself into the waves. Sally's most conservative bikini was made of shiny copper material and skimmed her nipples with minimal decency. But at least it was not a thong.

It turned out to be quite comfortable to swim in. Bella did not let herself think whether she would be equally comfortable to be seen in it. No, correct that: for *Gil* to see her in it.

She could not understand herself. She had danced and posed and sunbathed in provocative gear all her adult life. She had never felt this weird, shivering at the thought of just one person seeing her in *anything*. Yet the prospect of Gil returning from his marathon swim and finding her in Sally's high-fashion swimwear made her go hot and cold and want to turn for the hills.

Or alternatively stay and see what happened.

I must be out of my mind, thought Bella. In her agitation, she got her breathing wrong and sank. She emerged, spluttering.

When at last she got her breath back and opened her salt-stinging eyes, the dark speck was no longer heading for the horizon. It was about three feet away from her. And grinning like a devil.

'Knew you couldn't resist it in the end,' said Gil.

And kissed her.

It was like drowning. It was like flying. It was total sensation. It was beyond thinking. Beyond any further moves in any hypothetical game.

And, she suddenly realised, it was for ever. 'I love you,' said Bella, shaken.

But it was soundless and Gil's eyes were closed. He did not hear.

Just as well, thought Bella, pulling herself together, though her body still trembled in his arms. The sea pushed and nudged at them like a playful animal. Gil gave a husky laugh and opened his eyes.

'We're going to drown if we stay here.'

I think I just did.

'Not a good idea,' agreed Bella ambiguously.

She let him lead her out of the sea but detached herself as soon as they were on the beach, towelling herself with such concentration that she nearly took the skin off. Then she pulled her shirt over the damp bikini and buttoned it up to the throat.

'Does the winch work or do we have to climb?' she asked. To her own ears her voice sounded false.

Gil looked at her narrowly. He did not attempt to touch her again.

After a moment he said levelly. 'It works. Let me show you.'

And he did. He helped her onto the little stage, showed her the lever to pull, and stepped back.

'I'll walk,' he said drily. 'Give us both a breathing space. We seem to need it.'

He was right. Of course he was right. But Bella went up on the winch alone shaking so hard that she had to lean against the retaining bar or her legs would have buckled.

When it got to the top, she raced for the camera. It was a sort of protection. If she could remind him—remind them both—that she was here on a professional assignment, maybe she could take some of the dangerous tension out of the day.

She couldn't of course. Her body was not fooled. Her body was trembling so hard that she could scarcely hold the camera steady when she went to the top of the cliff to meet him.

He came up the path slowly. He looked indescribably weary. Almost defeated. Bella could not bear it.

She said his name softly. It was a note she recognised. And so did he. His head came up, and he met her eyes, his own incredulous.

She took the photograph on pure reflex. Then, very carefully, she put the camera down and went towards him.

Gil stopped dead, watching her gravely. Bella swallowed. And began to unbutton the damp shirt.

His eyes flared.

They did not make it to the house.

CHAPTER TEN

AFTERWARDS, of course, it was not at all romantic. The reality of sweaty, dust-stained bodies was as nothing compared with the screaming embarrassment in her head. She had virtually jumped on him! After he had told her that he did not take sex lightly! What he must think of her!

And there was something wrong, she knew it. Gil kept looking at her, as if he was waiting for her to say something. What? thought Bella, almost hysterical. An apology.

As soon as she decently could, she escaped into her bedroom and closed the door firmly. He did not invade her privacy. She had known he would not. She was glad.

He was not out on the terrace or in the kitchen that evening, though. The music poured out into the scented night as it always did. The barbecue was alight as it always was. There were glasses on the marble table. But no Gil.

Bella called his name. No answer. Was he playing games? She called again, more loudly.

She thought there was a sound from the end of the garden, where the rose-covered perimeter wall was in darkness. He *was* playing games. Bella's feelings fluctuated dramatically. She decided anger was safest. So, lips folded together, she marched down the path towards the sound.

There was a door in the wall she had not seen before. She pushed it open.

'Gil?' She did not sound quite as angry as she would have liked to. Or as confident.

A light wavered. Bella narrowed her eyes. He came to her out of the darkness. She held her breath.

But when he spoke, it was the most prosaic stuff.

'Did I alarm you? Sorry. The calor-gas cylinder is lower than I thought. And Jorgo didn't leave the new one where I asked him to. I thought he might have put it down here in the garage but he hasn't. I'm afraid we'll lose all power this evening.'

'Power?'

He lifted the torch he was holding. 'Yes. We're a long way from mains electricity here, you know. The radio and CD player work off batteries but light and heat are gas powered. No more hot showers until I get a replacement cylinder, I'm afraid. And you'll be going to bed by candlelight.'

'Cool,' said Bella. It came out a lot huskier than she'd meant.

As they walked back to the house, the terrace lights flickered out.

'There they go,' said Gil, resigned.

He put his arm round her. To steady her, presumably. He pointed the torch ahead of them at the uneven path, anyway. In the darkness, his body felt like warm rock at her shoulder.

Bella had a sudden inner vision. This was the man he should have been, the man he really was. Not the cyber millionaire she was here to interview. Not even the edgy genius who had possibly, probably, fallen in love with Annis. This was a man who knew about the practicalities of survival. He had the sustaining strength of one of his own olive trees. Not massive but enduring.

And he did not have enough passion in his life. Maybe she could give it to him. Maybe, in spite of the differences between them, maybe simple feeling could carry them through. She was in love, after all. She knew that now. Love counted for something, didn't it?

She said, 'I wish you would make love to me, Gil.'

It was meant to be an invitation but for some reason it sounded ineffably sad.

Gil stopped dead. His arm fell.

'Oh, Bella,' he said, as if it was wrenched out of him. 'I know it must sound stupid to you. But sex is more than fun to me. As long as there's someone else in the picture, I just can't.'

She thought she would die, it hurt so much. Suddenly it didn't matter if it was Annis or someone she had never heard of. There was a woman in his heart and in his memory that Bella could never oust, no matter what she did. Love was no use against a rival like that.

She gave up then.

He must have felt her reaction because he said quite kindly 'Don't worry about it.'

But he did not put his arm round her again. He did not touch her at all that night or for the rest of their time together on the island.

But he was a civilised man and he still made civilised conversation. Every word went through her like a knife but Bella lifted her chin and pretended that she did not care. For the two remaining nights, she fenced with him on the terrace in the starlight and then retreated to her solitary bed and lay wide awake until the dawn, agonised.

Just once, he tried to open the subject again.

It was on the last night. The angel voice was singing a playful, sexy little song about his lady love's beautiful mouth and the way she said yes.

Bella knew that was what it was about. She knew that CD insert off by heart now.

Gil looked up from the wine he was not drinking and said with difficulty, 'Bella—we have a problem. I want to be honest with you. There's no future for us until this other love—whatever it is—is well and truly in the past. Can you see that?'

She shrugged. 'You don't have to tell me that.'

She thought he flinched. 'No, I suppose not.'

The dancing little tune was suddenly unbearable. She got up.

'So that adds up to no future at all, I think. Probably just as well. We're not exactly soul mates, are we? I think I'll go to bed now. It's a long journey tomorrow.'

And she fled.

It was a relief to get back to work. In three days she had the story on her editor's desk.

Rita Caruso was pleased with the diary of the millionaire's island, ecstatic with the photographs for some reason, although Bella knew that her lack of expertise showed badly. Caruso was less pleased with the covering copy.

'Where are the secrets?' she demanded. 'You were there for a week. He must have told you something.'

'No.'

Caruso narrowed her eyes at her. 'What?'

'Nothing.'

'Did you have an affair with him?'

Bella was silent just fractionally too long. 'Of course not.'

'You did. Great. That's exactly what we need. You can gloss the diary. But at night we—'

'*No*,' shouted Bella, jumping to her feet.

Caruso was suddenly steely. 'You want that job when your secondment is over?'

She did. Oh, she did. She needed it. The only thing that was going to get her through this awfulness was a job she could immerse herself in. But not if it meant betraying Gil.

'Not at that price,' said Bella quietly.

'Then get out. You're fired.'

Bella nodded. Under the shocked eyes of the other people at the meeting, she stood up, gathered her notes and left.

'Excuse me,' said Sally diving after her.

The fellowship of the workplace locked into place at once. Three of them took her to lunch.

'You don't want to listen to Caruso. She fires everyone at least three times,' said one.

'She'll be calling you in to cancel before the day's out,' offered another.

'Can't you compromise?' suggested Sally. 'Meet her half way? I mean, you must have had a passionate kiss in the moonlight *once*. That gear I ordered up for you. No man would be able to keep his hands off that.'

'No,' said Bella with resolution.

Sally bit back a smile. But she said, 'OK. Your funeral.'

So Bella was packing her personal effects into an old photocopier-paper box, when she registered that a hush had fallen on the room.

Caruso coming back to put the boot in for a second time, she thought wearily. She turned, bracing herself.

'It's all right. I'm packing up—'

And broke off.

It was Gil de la Court. He was in his city suit again but somehow she did not see it. She only saw the golden brown eyes. They looked very serious.

He got to her desk, took the box away from her and took both her hands in a strong clasp.

'Bella Carew, you're a crazy, complicated deceptive woman. I don't care if you still think you're in love with another man. I know you're not. You may be in mourning for your lost childhood, but we can deal with that. This thing between us is too good to let it go for a fantasy. Will you marry me?'

It was well reasoned. He had been polishing it for days. Unfortunately, it sounded like it. Fluent and convincing though the argument was, it did not sound as if his heart was in it. Not to Bella anyway.

The drama was great though. The room held its collective breath.

Bella felt as if she was in a dream: a cruel dream where someone was offering her heart's desire just before the devil jumped out of his box crying, Fooled you!

She said roughly, 'Don't talk nonsense.'

'It's not nonsense. This is the most important thing I've ever done in my life.'

She tried to pull her hands away. He would not let her.

'Stop it,' she hissed under her breath.

Gil was imperturbable. 'Marry me.'

For a moment she almost hated him. 'Look, I've had all I can take from you,' she said, her voice breaking. 'Falling in love was bad enough. How much grief do I need? I've *done* embarrassment. I've done stupidity. I've done falling in love with men who want a class act like my sister.'

He was so startled, he loosened his clasp.

'Thank you,' Bella said, wrenching her hands away. She began to retreat.

'Bella—' he was very calm '—this will be the third time you have walked away from me. If you turn your back on me now, it will be down to you. I won't come after you again. If you want me, you'll have to come to me.'

It was too much. Bella could not bear it.

'Go away,' she yelled.

And ran.

'You're crazy, English,' said Sally in the ladies' rest room. 'He's gorgeous. He's sexy. He wants you so bad he's willing to make an idiot of himself in front of half a dozen hungry journalists. What more do you want?'

'I want him to love me,' said Bella, blotting her eye make-up ineffectually.

Sally raised her eyes to the ceiling. 'What on earth makes you think he doesn't love you? The guy came rushing round here. He had to walk out of some meeting with hotshot bankers but did he hesitate? No. He dropped everything the moment I called him.'

'You called him?'

'Of course.'

'But—'

'Someone has to make sure you don't junk the best thing that's ever likely to happen to you,' said Sally brutally.

'What do you mean, the best thing that ever happened to me? He was just an assignment...'

'Oh, yeah? An assignment whose photograph you carry around in your bag!'

'What?'

'All creased too. Look at it a lot, do you?'

All the fight went out of Bella. Suddenly she was trembling. 'You didn't tell him that, did you?' she pleaded.

Sally looked down her nose. '*I* didn't tell him. But you're a fool if *you* don't.'

'I *can't*. He's in love with someone else.'

'Oh, sure. Like that's why he came in and asked you to marry him in front of twenty witnesses.'

'But—'

'If you ask me,' said Sally, 'it sounded more as if he thought *you* were in love with someone else.'

Bella stared. Suddenly she heard that neat little speech in her head again. *'You still think you're in love with another man.'* Was it possible?

'Do you think so?' she said, hardly daring to hope.

'If I were you, I'd let Caruso think she's succeeded in firing you and get on the first plane to England,' advised Sally. 'Go see him. Find out.' She paused. 'You do know where he lives?'

Bella felt as if she had jumped off a cliff, shocked and winded but somehow, unexpectedly, alive. 'Er—Cambridge somewhere. I can find out. My sister will know.'

'Great,' said Sally, crumpling up the piece of paper in her pocket on which Gil had thoughtfully written his address. 'Go get him, tiger!'

The cottage was set back from the road, behind a hedge that needed cutting. Now she was here, Bella parked the car and sat behind the wheel for a bit, trying to get up her courage. A tangle of roses wafted in the long shadows of the summer twilight. There was a reading lamp on in one of the windows. So he was in.

Now she was here, she did not feel nearly as sure of herself. Gil might think this was an invasion of his privacy. He might have someone else with him. He might—

But there was no point sitting here, panicking about it. She had come here to do something and she had better pull herself together and get on with it. She got out of the racy sports car that had been her stepfather's last birthday present without even looking at it and squared her shoulders.

She got herself up the untidy front path by dint of concentrating on the overpowering scent of lavender. Once there, Bella swallowed. She wished it was still winter and she had her thick coat to hug round her. But it was summer and all she had was a big Thai-silk scarf. And she didn't really need that, except for courage.

She swallowed again and rang the bell.

Gil opened the door. He looked terrible. She realised she had never seen him unshaven before. His shirt was unbuttoned and there were ink stains on the flapping cuffs. His eyes looked bloodshot and weary. He stared at her for an unsmiling moment.

'May I come in?' she said in a small voice.

For a moment he did not answer. Then he shrugged and stood aside.

There were papers all over the floor. An open bottle of whisky sat in the middle of them. There was no glass. It looked as if he had been drinking straight from the bottle. Clever, controlled Gil de la Court, swigging from a bottle like a frontier desperado? Bella could not believe it.

She cleared her throat. 'I think I owe you an apology.'

Stupid. *Stupid.* Couldn't she think of anything better than that to say?

He shrugged again, turning away.

'Don't worry about it. You don't want to marry me. It's not your fault. You can't love two people at the same time.'

Bella stepped in front of him.

'Exactly. That's what I've been afraid of.'

He blinked. She could see the undisguised bewilderment.

'What?'

'I thought,' she said loudly, 'that you were in love with Annis.'

He seemed to come alive at that. *'What?'*

Bella quailed a little. 'My mother. And, well it seemed likely. You said she taught you about body language,' she said, not very coherently. 'And she's so clever. I mean, you'd have been well-suited. And I'm not clever at all…'

'Are you telling me,' he said with dangerous quietness, 'that you have put us through all this because you're jealous of *Annis*?'

'She's wonderful,' said Bella, firing up.

'Of course she's wonderful,' he said, impatient. 'She probably saved my business and she's a warm and wonderful person. But look at you. You stop traffic.'

And quite suddenly the thing that still stung, that had lodged like the poisoned dart, shot out, startling her almost as much as Gil.

'I didn't stop *you*,' her hurt heart said bitterly.

'What are you talking about?'

'You left me. That first morning. We'd made love but you went and didn't come back. And when you saw me you didn't even kiss me.'

Gil dropped his head in his hands. 'Oh, God, help me.'

'Why did you do that? It made me feel so lonely,' said Bella, forced into honesty

He dropped his hands. He looked almost wild for a moment.

'I shouldn't be let out alone. How could I have been so stupid? Bella, my love, I told you I didn't read women. I wouldn't have hurt you for the world. But I thought you would want your—space.'

'Why?' said Bella, bewildered.

'Because that's what I'd been taught,' said Gil grimly. 'I told you there was a woman a long time ago. I was an "A" student, she was a drop-out. She had a crazy, mixed-up history and I was the fall guy. Every time I held her she would fight me off saying I was trying to take her over. So I learned to keep my distance after we made love.'

'Oh,' said Bella. 'When you were a student?'

Not Annis, then. Not that it mattered now. Not the way he was looking at her.

'Yes. My friends will tell you that Rosemary was a manipulative tragedy queen with a bad case of self-dramatisation. I was very young. I thought she needed to be taken care of. And all I did was take on a lot of stupid ideas and use them to hurt you.' He looked remorseful. 'Will you ever forgive me?'

Bella hesitated. 'Did you ever want to take care of me?'

'Crazily enough, yes. After you fell asleep that night, I held you and promised myself that I would keep you safe. Getting up and leaving you alone the next morning was one of the most difficult things I'd ever done in my life. But I thought I owed it you not to crowd you.'

'Ah,' said Bella. 'I'm not so easily crowded, you know.'

Suddenly Gil was very close. 'Yes, I know. You're a wonder.'

She stood very still. He took another step towards her. They were almost touching.

'You dance like a demon. You meet life head-on. I've never seen such passion.'

'Oh!'

'And you make love with your whole heart.'

She was silenced.

'I need that,' said Gil quietly. 'I need you. I know that I'm a dull mathematician but you could change that.'

Bella began to smile. She could not help herself.

'Really?'

'Really. Ever since you told me about Kosta I've been torn between wanting to tear his liver out and give him a medal. I'm so glad that he turned you down. But I know he's made you cautious about any more risks. And I really need you to take a risk on me.'

'Ah,' said Bella.

She let the Thai shawl fall at last. It pooled across the disaster area of the floor. She did not notice. She stepped towards him.

'Do you think you ever could?' Gil said soberly. 'Eventually?'

She took his hand and helped him to slip one of the fashionable boot-lace straps off her shoulder.

'Since you mention it…'

His eyes widened. He took her by the shoulders. She could feel his hands shaking. He peeled the little black dress away in one uncontrolled movement.

'Bella,' he said, moved. 'My darling.'

She went into his arms, smiling, utterly confident.

'Lucky chap?' she asked.

She was laughing into his mouth as he tumbled her to the floor and the disaster area turned into heaven.

'Oh, by the way,' he said, a long time later, 'a fax came for you.'

Bella was resting her head on his shoulder in blissful content but she raised it at this.

'For me? Here? But nobody knew I was coming…'

'Someone called Caruso knew. She doesn't like the ending of some piece you've written. She wants you to change it.'

'But she fired me.'

'That isn't how it reads,' said Gil. He reached round her head and plucked it from his desk above their head.

Bella read it quickly.

'It looks like I've got a career after all,' she said jubilantly.

'Wonderful,' he said into her hair.

'If I can find a high note to end on. Maybe I can't,' said Bella, struck with self-doubt.

'Then, let me inspire you,' said Gil calmly. He twitched the paper out of her hand. 'What's this article about?'

'You,' said Bella baldly.

'Oh.' He grinned. 'That's easy. Do you know *Jane Eyre*?'

'Yes,' said Bella, bewildered.

'Well? Do you remember the end?'

'No, I haven't read it since I was at school.' She was slightly annoyed. 'What's that got to do with anything?'

'Come with me,' he said, and led her into his book-filled bedroom.

Not just books. Bella looked round and saw, besides a massive bed, a new-looking television with a pile of videos still wrapped in Cellophane. She looked up, a question in her eyes.

'My local video store's recommendations on children's movies,' he explained, faintly embarrassed. 'I thought I'd better get in something that would make you feel at home before I came looking for you again.'

'So you would have come after me again? In spite of what you said?'

He put his arm round her and held her close. 'Couldn't have helped myself,' he said simply. He walked her to the book shelf. 'Now, *Jane Eyre*. And then I can get down to the serious business of telling you exactly how much I love you.'

CHAPTER ELEVEN

IT WAS the final editorial meeting on the July issue of *Elegance Magazine* and it was not going well. Rita Caruso had come in with a late bid for column inches to accommodate a three-thousand-word article that had overrun by fifty per cent and she was fighting like a tiger.

'I can't cut it. It's an award winner.'

'Since when has there been an award for schmaltz?' said the beauty editor. It was her column inches under dispute.

'What's wrong with schmaltz?' said Caruso. 'The readers laugh a bit, cry a bit, end up with a great fat smile on their faces. Beautiful!'

'Sounds good to me,' admitted the literary editor and, as the others all stared incredulously, said defensively, 'So I like a happy ending! What about it?'

Caruso beamed. 'And what an ending.' She pushed the page proof into the middle of the conference table. 'Just look at it!'

Several people leaned forward.

The literary editor, who had already read it, did not. He looked at Caruso curiously.

'It's by the English girl, right? I thought you weren't sure about her.'

'I'm sure. She's got a good ear and a nice way with words. My recommendation to take her on has been in London for months.'

'Really? The girls thought she was on some kind of make-or-break test with this one.'

Caruso smiled like a cat that had got the cream. 'It's called man-management, Freddy. And oh, boy, didn't it work?'

She glanced down at the page proof with maternal fondness.

She had used a dark brooding photograph, after Sally had tracked the photographer down and had done a deal with him. But the big, full-page picture was one of Bella's from Greece. It showed Gil coming up the cliff path after a swim. The light had been wonderful, throwing into bas-relief the sculptured muscles of shoulders and powerful legs.

But it wasn't the spare elegance of classical torso, nor the golden tan, nor even the sheer energy of movement that caught the attention. It was his expression. He had looked up at the last moment and had seen Bella taking the photograph. Even an unaccustomed photographer like Bella could not have messed that one up. His heart was in his eyes.

And then there was the sign-off line, of course. Not a sentimental woman, even Caruso admitted herself moved by that.

Bella had come awake with a jump.

'My deadline. When was it? What did you do with that bit of paper?'

Gil pulled her closer against his warm chest. 'I can't get up,' he said lazily. 'You'll feel rejected.'

'Don't tease me. This is serious. I might just have a career if I get back before the deadline.'

'Career women. No sense of priority.'

He stretched enjoyably and laughed as she could not control her little quiver of response.

'That's not fair. I've never had a career before,' she said. 'I want to do this properly.' But she turned in his arms and kissed him lingeringly before she got out of bed.

Pleased, he watched her pad naked across the floor between their strewn clothes. Rather more of his clothes than hers of course. His mouth curled irrepressibly at the memory.

He put his hands behind his head and leaned back with a sigh of contentment.

'I can see I'm going to be a neglected husband, fitted in between assignments,' he told the ceiling provocatively.

Bella came back with the crumpled page and his laptop computer.

'You're going to be a *supportive* husband,' she said firmly. She pushed the laptop across the covers to him. 'You'll have to set this up for me, genius.'

He laughed and dealt with the thing expertly. He did not get up but he rolled over on his stomach and reached out a long arm to plug it into the telephone socket beside the bed.

'You only want me for my computer skills,' he complained, righting himself.

Bella looked down at him with total love. 'I want you for every reason there is,' she said.

There was a long, complicated silence while he explored that statement. Eventually she emerged, wide-eyed and laughing, and smoothed her hair with rather shaky fingers.

'Of course the computer skills are a definite bonus.' The shared laughter was a marvel but it was just the surface of what she felt, like the spray that powered off the cliff-face of their island—spectacular but nothing compared with the depth of feeling underneath. She looked into his eyes. 'Love you,' she said, very quietly.

His hand closed on hers so hard it hurt.

But all he said was, 'Love you too. We do this thing together, right?'

He was talking about more than her assignment and they both knew it.

'Yes,' said Bella, very confidently.

But he was talking about her assignment as well, since the final contribution was his idea. So they sat side by side with the computer balanced precariously on her knee and typed in the message, taking alternate words.

There was a demarcation dispute over who typed the punctuation. But they settled that by a long, competitive kiss. It did not stay competitive but it did end up very long indeed. The screen had gone dark waiting for them to complete the sentence by the time Bella looked round for the computer again.

'Tsk,' said Gil, wickedly. 'Think of your career. Concentrate.'

Bella laughed. 'All right. I'll finish it. You send the email. Fair?'

'Agreed.'

She completed the message.

Delete and replace final paragraph, it read.

And two days later, the entire editorial team looked down at the new final paragraph and agreed that Caruso could have her column inches.

It said, Reader, I married him.